I0647622

POPULAR PUBLICATIONS — FACSIMILE EDITIONS

Dime Detective Magazine #2
(December 1931)

Dime Detective magazine was the flagship detective pulp in the Popular Publications stable, running for almost 300 issues over twenty years. The second issue contains stories by T.T. Flynn, Maxwell Hawkins, J. Allan Dunn, Frederick Nebel, and Erle Stanley Gardner, and includes another appearance by Nebel's long-running series character, Cardigan.

Authors:

*T.T. Flynn, Maxwell Hawkins, J. Allan Dunn,
Frederick Nebel, Erle Stanley Gardner*

Illustrators:

William Reusswig, Amos Sewell, John Fleming Gould

"I'll PROVE in Only 7 Days that I Can Make YOU a New Man!"

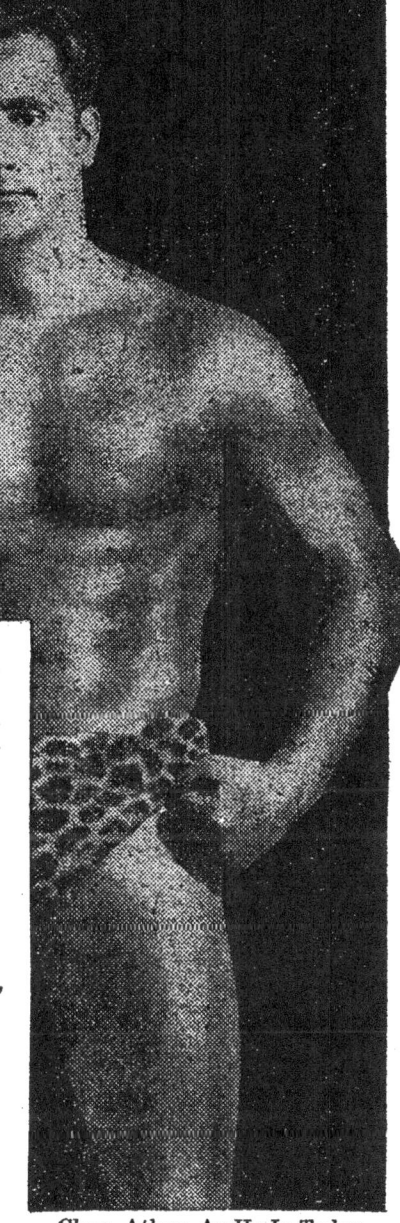

Chas. Atlas: As He Is Today.

No other Physical Instructor in the World has ever DARED make such an Offer!

By CHARLES ATLAS
Holder of the Title:
"The World's Most Perfectly Developed Man"

I HAVE proved to thousands that my system of building powerful, big-muscled men begins to show real results *in only 7 days*—and I can prove it *to you*.

You don't have to take my word for it. You don't have to take the word of my hundreds of pupils who have added inches to their chests, biceps, necks, thighs and calves in only a few days. No sir! You can prove for *yourself*—in just one week —by the change you see and *feel* in *your own body*—that you can actually become a husky, healthy NEW MAN—a real "Atlas Champion."

All I want to know is: Where do *you* want big, powerful muscles? How many pounds of firm flesh do *you* want distributed over your body to fill you out? Where do *you* lack vitality, pep and robust health? Where do *you* want to take off flabby surplus fat?

Just tell me, give me a week, and I'll show you that I can make a *New Man* of you, give you bodily power and drive, and put you in that magnificent physical condition which wins you the envy and respect of any man and the admiration of every woman.

My own system of *Dynamic-Tension* does it. That's the way I built myself from a 97-pound weakling to "The World's Most Perfectly Developed Man." And now *you* can have a big, balanced muscular development like mine in the same easy way.

No "Apparatus" Needed!

You begin to FEEL and SEE the difference in your physical condition at once, without using any tricky apparatus, any pills, "rays" or unnatural dieting. My *Dynamic-Tension* is a *natural* method of developing you *inside and out*. It not only makes you an "Atlas Champion," but goes after such ailments as constipation, pimples, skin blotches, and any other weaknesses that keep you from really enjoying life and its good times—and it starts getting rid of them at once.

Let Me Tell You How

Gamble a 2c stamp today by mailing the coupon for a free copy of my new illustrated book, *"Everlasting Health and Strength."* It tells you all about my special *Dynamic-Tension* method. It shows you, from actual photos, how I have developed my pupils to the same perfectly balanced proportions of my own physique, by my own secret methods. What my system did for me, and these hundreds of others, it can do for you too. Don't keep on being only 25 or 50 per cent of the man you *can* be! Find out what I can do for you.

FREE BOOK

Where shall I send your copy of "Everlasting Health and Strength?" Jot your name and address down on the coupon, and mail it today. Your own new "Atlas body" is waiting for you. This book tells you how *easy* it is to get, my way. Send the coupon to me personally—

CHARLES ATLAS
Dept. 10-M
133 E. 23rd St., New York City

1

Every Story Complete   *Every Story New*

Vol 1   CONTENTS *for* DECEMBER, 1931   *No.* 2

Watch for the January Issue   On the Newsstands Dec. 20th

Published every month by Popular Publications, Inc., North Broadway, Albany, New York. Editorial and executive offices 205 East 42nd Street, New York City. Harry Steeger, President and Secretary, Harold S. Goldsmith, Vice President and Treasurer. Application for second class entry pending at the Post Office at Albany, New York, under the Act of Congress, March 3, 1879. Title registration pending at U. S. Patent Office. Copyrighted 1931 by Popular Publications, Inc. Single copy price 10c. Yearly subscriptions in U. S. A. $1.00. For advertising rates address H. D. Cushing, 67 West 44th Street, New York, N. Y. When submitting manuscripts, kindly enclose sufficient postage for their return if found unavailable. The publishers cannot accept responsibility for return of unsolicited manuscripts, although all care will be exercised in handling them.

3

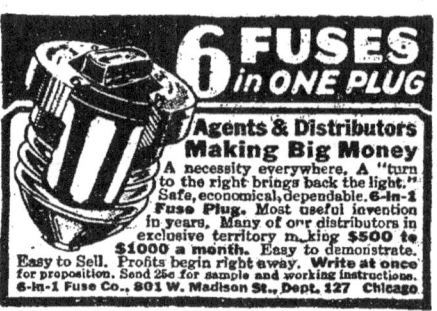

4

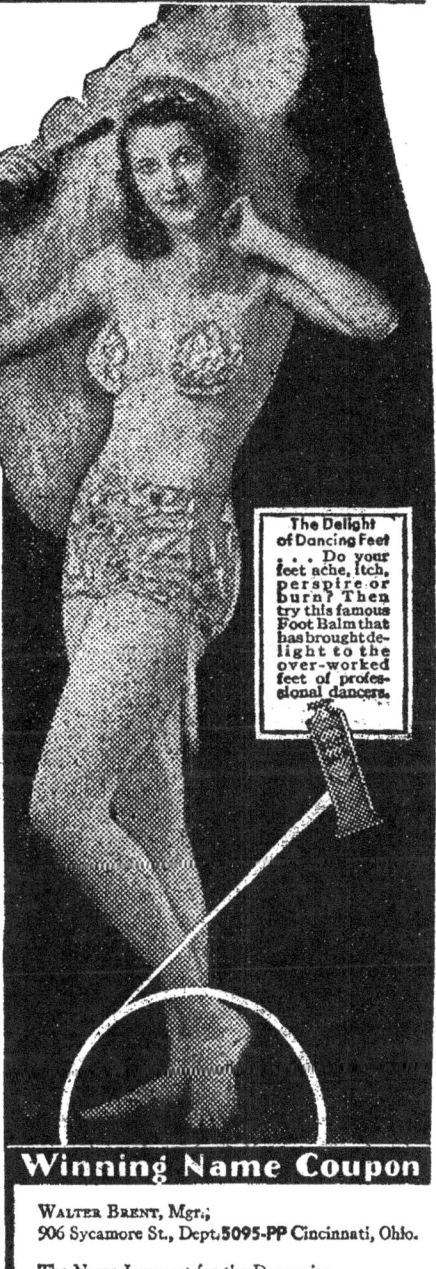
5

The Revel of Death

by T. T. Flynn

Author of "The Pullman Murder," etc.

A scream of fright and terror from the woman's throat—"Murder! Come quick!"

Laughter and mad music on the tropic night—the surge of masked dancers in festive revel. And in an upstairs room before an opened safe Death lurked to strike down Satan and his twin.

CHAPTER ONE

Satan and Co.

MUSIC was throbbing on the soft Florida night as Jim Reilly stepped out of the long black roadster, adjusted the flaming scarlet cloak about his shoulders and said to Patsy Peters: "Pass me that pitchfork."

Patsy Peters thrust out the three-pronged trident and slid nimbly from the seat, standing short and sinister in his sooty make-up as an imp of the nether regions.

"How do I look?" Jim Reilly asked him.

"Like hell," said Patsy critically, and amplified it immediately. "I mean, you look like you're hot out of hell."

And in truth there was a touch of the malevolent and sinister about the tall scarlet figure of Satan standing there under the Japanese lanterns, sharp trident in hand, red tail dangling, blunt horns protruding above the red leering devil's mask.

"I guess we'll both get by," Jim Reilly chuckled. "Let's take a walk around the island and see how everything stacks up before we go in."

He started to turn away as another car rolled into the parking space next to them. Started to turn—and Patsy grabbed him, stopped him at the risk of rending good cloth.

"Say!" Jim Reilly hissed through the red mask as he wheeled around. "What's the idea of yanking my tail? I thought I told you not to drink this evening?"

"Haven't had a drop!" Patsy denied just as indignantly. "Turn your back to that car! 'Beef' Miller and another dick are getting out of it! He had his mask off when he went by!"

Jim Reilly turned quickly and thrust his head inside the roadster, ostensibly looking for something. Through the windshield he surveyed the two men getting out of the car.

They were both stocky men, wearing Pierrot costumes. One of them was adjusting his mask as they walked heavily toward the big house from which music and sounds of gaiety were issuing.

Jim Reilly straightened up, looked after them thoughtfully. Patsy came out from behind the car where he had ducked.

Jim Reilly said: "You're right! Look at them walk! Picking them up and laying them down like they're still on night beats. Nothing but a pair of dressed-up harness bulls."

"Beef Miller's got more brains than a whole platoon of harness bulls," Patsy remarked, the whites of his eyes rolling through the eyeholes of his black mask.

"Blast him, he has!" Jim Reilly admitted.

"I wonder what they're doing here," Patsy said anxiously.

"Sifting the guests."

"Maybe we'd better stay clear of the place tonight," Patsy muttered.

Jim Reilly chuckled softly. "Forget 'em."

"You told me to forget that boil on my shoulder, and then you forgot and slapped it."

"I apologized," Jim Reilly chuckled as they walked away from the roadster.

"Yeah," Patsy grumbled. "You apologized, but the boil didn't pay any attention."

Poinsettia Island was a blaze of light, color and activity this evening. For the Rodney Dorringtons were giving their annual mid-season ball. Giving it with all the splendor and lavishness for which they were famous.

Across the velvet sweep of Biscayne Bay the city of Miami sprawled like a light-spangled backdrop. Red, green, blue lights; and strings, festoons and columns of white lights twinkling like crystal points against the soft semi-tropic night. And on Poinsettia Island, one of the small artificial islands dredged out of Biscayne Bay, surrounded by water on three sides, strings of gay Japanese lanterns festooned the lawn about the big white coral home of the Dorringtons. Automobiles were rolling in, discharging their masked and costumed passengers and parking. Now and then a launch slid up to the lighted boat landing at the side of the house, tied up and discharged passengers also.

It was a gorgeous night; stars winking through the palms; the moon not yet up from the open sea beyond Miami Beach. A night of splendor, of gaiety. The papers had been writing about the ball for a week. The wealth that would shortly be congregated in the house was staggering.

The guest list was large—and it was going to be larger, for the names of Jim Reilly and Patsy Peters were not included. Which did not worry them in the slightest.

One thing worried them however. As they left the lighted parking space, a slender figure slipped from the depths of a dark sedan near the end and flitted after them, keeping in the shelter of such bushes as were available.

Jim Reilly was humming softly under his breath as he and Patsy strolled along the palm-fringed walk and looked down at the dark water lapping restlessly against the sheer rock wall which formed the edge of the man-made island.

Patsy was silent, moving like a black shadow beside him.

THEY came to the boathouse and the small jetty thrusting out into the water. Half a dozen smart craft were moored there. A burly, middle-aged man with a nautical cast to his jib seemed to have charge of them.

Jim Reilly and Patsy went on.

And after them came the slender figure, walking casually, taking clever advantage of every bit of cover.

Beyond the boathouse the shadows grew thicker and there was an extended cluster of bushes flanking the curving path. As the first turn swallowed them Jim Reilly stopped, turned, peered back at the lighted area before the boathouse.

"What's the matter?" Patsy asked under his breath.

Jim Reilly's hand clamped on Patsy's arm in silent warning. Patsy stood like a black statue.

Light quick steps crunched softly on the shell path. Jim Reilly melted back in the bushes, pulling Patsy after.

A dark, slender figure came to the spot where they had been standing, saw the path was empty, stopped and listened, peering ahead in the thick shadows.

Jim Reilly stepped out, leaving Patsy still in the bushes.

The slender figure whirled quickly at the sound, uttered a little gasp of surprise at the sight of the wiry, diabolical figure that had so suddenly materialized.

"Looking for someone?" Jim questioned through his mask.

A moment's silence followed.

He was looking at a woman, dressed in the bulky skirts, the tight braided jacket, the winged cap of a Dutch milkmaid. Her soft arms were bare, two thick yellow braids fell down to her waist.

And when she spoke her voice had the faintest trace of an accent that could never be Dutch. Soft, limpid, liquid; perhaps a disguise for her true voice.

"So you came after all?"

"I'm here," Jim Reilly agreed cautiously.

"After the warning you got?"

"Did you send me a warning?"

"I did!" she snapped impatiently.

"Why?"

Anger seemed to be growing in her. "Why do you stand there and waste words? You know why! There must not be killing tonight!"

And in those last vehement words Jim Reilly read an earnestness that snapped him into wariness. He asked after a moment: "Why were you following me?"

"I thought you would pay no attention to my message. I have been watching for your devil's suit to show up. And when you didn't go straight to the house I followed you to see what you were up to. Where is the little man who came with you?"

"Back in the bushes," Jim Reilly told her.

"Who is he? Sanchez?"

"No."

"Who?"

"What does it matter?"

"It doesn't," she agreed—and a stray beam of light from the boat landing showed her mouth going tight beneath the edge of her mask. A small mouth, heavily rouged, with a well-formed chin under it. What little of her skin he could see was smooth and firm. She was young and—Jim was ready to wager—pretty. His interest flamed. Mystery here. And tense, dramatic, dangerous mystery by her words.

She had asked if Patsy was Sanchez. That was a Spanish name. She must be Spanish too.

"Well?" she asked impatiently.

"Well," Jim answered gravely.

"What are you going to do?"

"How do I know?" he countered.

"Are you going in the house?"

"I suppose so, as long as I'm here."

"I'll be watching."

"I can't think of anything better," Jim chuckled softly. "Perhaps you'll give me a dance?"

"You?" The haughty lift to her head was answer enough for that; and then her manner changed instantly. "Perhaps I might," she agreed hurriedly, turning away.

"Wait," Jim protested. "Better go in with us?"

"I won't be seen with you—out here."

"Inside then?" Jim suggested.

She paused, peering at him. "You are either a fool, or a very reckless man," she snapped, and was gone as quickly as she had appeared.

Jim Reilly stood in the path looking after her.

Patsy Peters edged out of the bushes. "Who is that dame?" he demanded suspiciously.

Jim Reilly shrugged. "You heard her, didn't you?"

"I heard her," Patsy agreed. "Is she cuckoo, talking about a killing tonight?"

"No," said Jim thoughtfully. "I don't think she is. There's something in the wind, Patsy. Something bad."

"What's it got to do with us?"

"I'm wondering," Jim Reilly said slowly. "And I've got a hunch we're going to be tangled in it some way. Let's go in the house and see."

THERE was music in the front part of the big house; music and life and gaiety. And there were a few lights at the back too, and orderly bustle among the servants. Bustle that stopped momentarily, became surcharged with interest as the screen door was opened and the tall scarlet-clad figure of Satan stalked into the big kitchen, followed by the sooty figure of an imp.

The imp winked at a comely housemaid, who simpered.

The devil paused in the middle of the kitchen and haughtily surveyed the peering servants, half of whom turned guiltily back to their work.

"One of you bring me a drink," the devil ordered huskily from behind the leering mask.

A white-hatted chef shrugged his shoulders with Gallic agreement and said briskly: "*Oui*, Monsieur Dorrington. Suzette, a drink for Monsieur Dorrington at once. The punch is in the icebox."

"Eh?" said the devil harshly. "What's that?"

"Immediately, monsieur," the chef bobbed. "Suzette, *allez vite!*"

Suzette, chic and pretty in a white apron and cap, was already opening the enameled door of a huge icebox. Her deft fingers whisked out a glass of frosty liquid and brought it to the scarlet figure.

"Make it two, kid," the sooty imp suggested; and forthwith grunted with pain as the scarlet devil kicked him none too gently on the ankle.

"Lay off the rough stuff!" the imp breathed in anguish. "You like to broke my hoof then!"

"Ixnay, you idiot!" the devil hissed between sips. "Close that trap of yours before I paste it shut with a handful of dough off the table there!"

The swift interchange of low-voiced remarks apparently attracted no attention. Beaming, the chef rubbed his hands together and queried: "Monsieur approves the punch?"

Suzette had placed a second frosty glass in the hands of the imp, who drained half of it and smacked his lips as he replied to the chef: "Both monseers do, Henri! It's great!"

The chef bowed. "Philippe is the name, monsieur," he corrected.

"Rudolph, you're drunk again," the scarlet-clad Satan spoke curtly, whisking the glass out of the imp's fingers. "The punch is excellent, Philippe."

And as the chef beamed his thanks, a firm grasp propelled the sooty imp out of the kitchen, through a butler's pantry and a small hall into a sizeable dining room which was vacant at the moment.

"You idiot!" Jim Reilly hissed as they stopped beyond the door. "What's the idea of coming into the kitchen and acting like a lowbrow who's trying to date one of the maids?"

Patsy Peters shrugged sulkily. "I saw you kidding 'em and thought I'd get in on the fun."

"That wasn't fun," Jim snorted. "I made them run for a drink so they'd have an idea we belonged inside. And that chef called me Dorrington!"

"Huh?"

"Dorrington. Get it? Dorrington! He thought I was the boss. That means Dorrington is dressed like a devil too. We're about the same build. They couldn't tell the difference. What a break!"

"Gosh!" Patsy breathed. "Break is right. What do we do? Step in and run the party?"

"We step in and see what's going on," Jim Reilly said shortly. "And don't forget we're walking on eggs. Anything can happen tonight. There are two dicks here that we know about, and someone has got murder on her mind. We're lucky if we get away with our skins. Come on."

CHAPTER TWO

Borrowed Brimstone

THE two of them were silent and watchful as they walked through the dining room and across a hall into a large, brightly lighted room banked with flowers and filled with costumed guests. An orchestra behind a screen of small potted palms was playing; couples were dancing on the highly waxed floor; around the edges of the room people were sitting, standing, talking.

Jim Reilly bore to the left, mingled with the guests quickly.

"Drift," he said to Patsy quickly. "Circulate around the room the other way. Keep your eyes open. Look for a chap dressed like me. And watch for those two dicks."

Patsy nodded, parted from him there. Patsy could be stupid at times, but also when necessary he could do what he was told quickly, efficiently.

Jim Reilly moved along the edge of the dance floor, eyeing the guests. Imaginations had run riot and rampant this evening. There were plump colonial dames and spare pilgrim fathers, painted Indians, Spanish dons and senoritas, Greeks and Chinese. A Cleopatra displayed more skin than clothing. A lusty pirate or two swaggered in soft leather boots, bright kerchiefs, pistols and knives.

How many were present it was hard to guess. The room was crowded, more guests were arriving every moment. Reilly looked for another Satan and failed to see him.

A glance into the large entrance hall showed two Pierrots unobtrusively scanning the guests who entered. A powdered and wigged footman was at the door taking up invitation cards.

At that sight Jim Reilly was thankful that they had managed to get in from the rear. It was just such a barrier that he had tried to avoid after failing to secure admission cards for himself and Patsy.

One of the Pierrots noticed his presence in the doorway and came quickly toward him. Jim Reilly throttled an impulse to retreat hastily and waited.

"Everything seems to be all right so far, Mr. Dorrington," the detective said under his breath. "Everyone who has come in since we've been here has a card."

The man's mask did not fully hide a short stubby iron-gray mustache, thick strong lips and an undershot jaw.

Beef Miller, it was, from Miami police headquarters. Beef Miller who for twenty years had worked out of Center Street in New York. Beef Miller, in whose camera mind were filed the features and records of most of the well-known criminals of North America.

Twice in the past he had placed handcuffs on the very wrist that now held the three-pronged trident. And it wasn't Beef Miller's fault that each time the evidence had been insufficient for a conviction.

It had not set well with Beef Miller. The second time he had seen his prisoner walk debonairly out of the courtroom, he had waylaid him in a corridor and promised angrily to make no mistake the third time.

Patsy had come under his notice too.

But all that had happened several years back—in New York. Since then Beef Miller had retired from the cold winters and blustery blizzards of the North and bestowed his presence on sunny Miami. There a place had quickly been made for him on the headquarters staff. A man who knew as many criminals as Beef Miller was invaluable. For more and more they too were following the flight of money and comfort South during the winter months.

BEEF MILLER met the trains, strolled through the hotels, walked the streets, routing unwelcome tourists through the mill at headquarters. Some were warned out of town, some allowed to stay; and if there was trouble Beef Miller went through the roster of those present in this territory and very often found the wanted man.

And here was Beef Miller standing before him, speaking with a deference he had never displayed before to Jim Reilly.

Behind the leering satanic mask, Jim smiled wryly. "Good," he grunted throatily. "Keep it up."

"We'll do that, Mr. Dorrington," Beef Miller said deferentially, turning away.

With a breath of relief Jim Reilly continued his promenade. It had been a strain standing there with nothing but a thin piece of cloth between his features and the searching glance of Beef Miller.

A few minutes later he saw Patsy dancing with the shapely, bare-limbed figure of Cleopatra. When the dance was over Jim waylaid his partner and spoke to him sternly.

"You would get tangled up in the first pair of legs that ran in front of you!" he said. "Lay off that, stupid! Move around. Keep your eyes open. We've got to work quick! As soon as Beef Miller and that sidekick of his get wise to the fact that there are two devils who look exactly alike they'll begin to get curious. And if they start asking questions they're liable to find out that Beef Miller wasn't talking to Dorrington a few minutes ago, as he thought he was. Then it'll be time to lift masks and our geese'll be cooked. Get me?"

Patsy grumbled defensively: "Ain't I been dancin' around the room tryin' to find out where that Dutch milkmaid dame is who was talkin' to us outside?"

For the moment Jim Reilly had forgotten her. After all she was more or less unimportant beside the things which had brought them here. But now he frowned behind his mask. "Seen anything of her?" he asked.

"Nope."

"Keep your eyes open. I'm going upstairs."

"You know where to go yet?" Patsy demanded.

"I'll have that fellow with the tray take me up and show me."

Jim Reilly indicated one of the powdered, bewigged footmen in knee breeches, who was offering to the various guests along the edge of the dance floor a silver tray laden with glasses of punch.

Patsy's jaw dropped. "You're gonna what?"

"Have that fellow take me up."

"If I had your nerve," Patsy sighed admiringly, "I'd be the Duke of Africa by next Saturday." And Patsy turned away, shaking his head.

But before Jim Reilly got to the footman a large dowager-type female in a colonial dame's costume sailed past a group of laughing guests a yard or so away and called imperiously: "Rodney!"

The name failed to click for an instant. Jim walked on.

"Rodney!" Impatient fingers gripped his arm, stopped him. The broad-bosomed colonial dame confronted him, demanding impatiently: "Where have you been, Rodney?"

For an instant Jim Reilly was at a loss for words. He realized that his costume had again mixed up things. This woman knew him, thought he was Dorrington. He stalled lamely. "Why —er—outside."

"Outside in the shadows with some young hussy, I suppose! I saw Loretta Kincaid go outside a few minutes ago! I know her in spite of that costume! So that's where you were!"

With a shock Jim Reilly realized who this woman was. Rodney Dorrington's wife! His wife now if the deception was to be kept up.

He felt a cold dew of perspiration

breaking out on his forehead. It was a little more than he had bargained for. Beef Miller was one thing. Rodney Dorrington's wife in the flesh was another.

For a moment Jim almost wished the real Rodney Dorrington would appear. He debated the advisability of assuring her that he was merely one of the guests. And then the thought of the consequences stopped him. Rodney Dorrington's wife seemed a determined woman. One who might be inquisitive, who might make trouble.

He said nothing.

"So that's what you were doing!" Rodney Dorrington's wife declared triumphantly.

"No, my dear," Jim answered throatily.

"What is the matter with your voice, Rodney?"

"Nothing."

"You sound guilty," she sniffed.

"No, my dear."

"Why are you calling me 'my dear'? You never did before. I suppose you think I'm that Kincaid hussy? Or that you can pull the wool over my eyes with soft words! Well, you can't!"

Jim Reilly felt himself sinking into the mire of complications. For a moment he almost felt sorry for Rodney Dorrington, in spite of what he knew about the man.

"Where did you get that ridiculous trident?" his spouse by proxy asked.

"It's a surprise," Jim Reilly mumbled.

"You look silly carrying it around. Put it away. Leave it upstairs in the bedroom before you come down."

"The bedroom?" Jim Reilly gulped.

"Yes. Come upstairs with me."

"Er—really, I'd rather not right now," Jim protested feebly.

"Rodney! Come upstairs with me!"

"Later."

"Rodney, are we going to have a scene right here before everyone? I want you to come upstairs at once!"

JIM REILLY turned a hunted glance around the room. There was no succor in sight. And then he stiffened. Not a dozen yards away stood the slender figure of a Dutch milkmaid. Her eyes were intently on him.

"Who is that girl dressed like a Dutch milkmaid?" Jim inquired of his companion.

A withering stare at the girl was followed by concentrated fury in the answer. "Another woman you're intending to run after?"

"I should say not!" Jim Reilly denied hastily.

"Don't tell me, Rodney Dorrington! I know you of old. Come upstairs with me!"

Suddenly behind his mask, Jim Reilly grinned. An idea had suddenly sprung into his mind. He wondered why he hadn't thought of it before. There was some luck in this encounter after all. Meekly, silently, he followed the imposing figure of Mrs. Rodney Dorrington into the large front hall, where a wide sweeping staircase led up to the second floor.

The two detectives were still on duty there. Jim beckoned to them. "Never mind watching the door any more," he directed. "Go in and mix among the guests."

"O. K, Mr. Dorrington," Beef Miller assented.

And as the detectives left the front hall Jim Reilly followed the costumed figure up the staircase.

In ominous silence she led the way into a big bedroom, lavishly done in pastel shades and ruffled lace. With a jerk she removed her mask, revealing the harsh, rather masculine features of a woman about fifty. She had a jaw as strong as a man's, a large nose, more than a suggestion of a dark mustache on her upper lip. Turning her back to him, she requested coldly: "Take off my necklace, Rodney. The clasp is scratching my neck. Some stupid oaf bumped against it and drew blood."

Jim looked, saw that she spoke the truth. Around her neck was a glittering, scintillating diamond necklace, with a diamond-set platinum clasp at the back. Beneath the clasp was an angry streak of red skin, faintly discolored with blood where the clasp had dug deeply.

Jim cast the trident on the bed, thankful for the red cotton gloves he was wearing. There would be no fingerprints on the trident handle when it was found there.

Deftly he unfastened the necklace, pausing for a moment to admire it.

"See if you can fix the clasp," Rodney Dorrington's wife snapped, turning around. "Don't stand there like a stupid lout! I must get downstairs."

"I'll fix it later, my dear," Jim suggested.

"Stop calling me 'my dear'! You never did that before! And I want it fixed now. I insist upon wearing it. It's the only distinguishing thing about this costume. Take your mask off. How can you see to do anything with it on?"

Jim Reilly saw it coming, was not quick enough to avert it. Her plump fingers caught the bottom of the scarlet mask, pulled it down, revealing his face.

And Jim acted with catlike speed. As her jaw dropped, her eyes widened with astonishment and fright and a scream welled into her throat. His hand clamped firmly over her mouth.

"Keep quiet!" he ordered sharply.

He was as kind as he could be. Rough tactics with women were not his way. He hadn't counted on anything like this, but as long as it had occurred it had to be met.

She struck at him. Muffled screams smothered against the palm of his hand. Jim forced her to the bed, set her down smartly on it.

"Will you be quiet?" he entreated. "I don't want to have to be rough."

The matter was solved for him. Rodney Dorrington's wife fainted. As her weight went limp in his grasp and the screams ceased Jim let her back on the bed and looked down at her regretfully.

"Sorry to frighten you this way, old girl," he murmured. "But after all I guess it won't do you any harm. Not after the way you evidently handle your husband."

With his mask in place again he glanced at the necklace briefly, slipped it in a pocket underneath his scarlet suit. And then he worked swiftly. Stripping off the two pillow cases he ruthlessly ripped them into strips, gagged and bound the still limp matron.

He lifted her, grunting a bit with the effort, for she was no lightweight, and carried her across the room to an open closet, deposited her on the floor and closed the door. There was a key in the lock. He turned it, took it over to the dressing table and slipped it under a hand mirror. And then he left the bedroom, closing the door behind him.

CHAPTER THREE

Death For The Devil

MUSIC, laughter, conversation and sounds of dancing poured up the stairway from below. The upper hall was empty for the moment.

Jim opened a door opposite, saw another bedroom with half a score of women's cloaks tossed across the bed. Three costumed women clustered around a dressing table turned quickly.

"Pardon me," Jim uttered hastily, and closed the door again, their titters following him.

He went back along the hall, glancing into door after door; and at the back found what he was searching for. A combined study and office, wholly masculine. The room was dark when he looked in; he found a light switch inside the door and pressed it.

A leather-covered couch stood against the wall; a table, light and comfortable reading chair in the middle of the floor. At one end of the room was a stone fireplace, at the other a desk. Etchings hung on the walls, and over a fireplace a big swordfish was mounted on a mahogany background.

Jim closed the door softly and scrutinized the room carefully. After a moment he walked across to the roll-top desk and tried to open it. It was locked.

He slipped a hand inside his scarlet suit and brought out a thin flat packet of soft leather. He opened it on top of the desk, revealing half a dozen tools, tied in place by black strings. He selected one, straightened it out and had a small steel jimmy.

Few people would have believed such a tool had cost as much as that jimmy had. There were only three places in the United States where one could buy such a tool, and this one had come from the best, Dooley in Philadelphia. It had the lightness of a feather, the strength of a crowbar.

Carefully Jim Reilly inserted the tool under the edge of the desk top, thrust it in gently and pried. The top yielded a trifle. From the kit he took a flat steel wedge and slipped it in the crack. Withdrawing the jimmy he inserted it again some inches nearer the lock and pried again. A final sharp pressure

brought a metallic snap as the lock broke. The top slid up.

Inside were papers, envelopes, documents, stuffed into pigeonholes. A swift methodical search took him through the lot in ten minutes, without reward.

Jim straightened, frowning behind his mask.

The desk had drawers on the right side, a single door on the left. Swiftly, expertly he broke the lock on that door, revealing the polished metal front of a small stout safe.

Jim replaced the kit under his suit, slowly drew the scarlet glove off the slender, tapering fingers, carefully manicured, of his right hand. He flexed the fingers experimentally, lifted a shoe and rubbed the tips hard for some seconds against the rough leather sole. Wiping the dirt off on his suit, he rubbed the thumb over the finger tips and dropped before the safe.

The closed door muffled the sounds from the lower part of the house. Ear close to the safe door, Jim Reilly turned the narrow combination knob delicately. No one but a master of his craft could have appreciated the skill of those movements. The experience of years was behind them. His body was like a taut violin string, every nerve straining for the movement behind that steel door.

The faintest click registered; the tiniest jar came up through his sensitive finger tips as one of the tumblers fell.

Jim worked on patiently, utterly oblivious to the face that Rodney Dorrington's wife might release herself or be found at any moment and his trespass discovered. And there again one found the training of years. Complete mastery over body, mind and senses.

The last tumbler clicked almost imperceptibly. His gloved hand turned the handle. The door swung out noiselessly.

Not until then did Jim take a long breath of relief, pull out a handkerchief and wipe his face under the mask. The strain had been terrific.

Drawing on the other glove, he went through the contents of the safe quickly. There were papers, sealed documents, several packets of securities and bonds. And one small drawer was crammed with bank notes of large denomination.

There were also several pieces of jewelry—an emerald bracelet, a diamond brooch, a pearl necklace. He disregarded them at the moment as he opened a large manila enevelope on which the letters M. B. were scrawled in purple ink.

The envelope was crammed with folded sheets of letter paper, some smudged, dirty, crinkled, as if they had been carried for a long time. Jim glanced at one or two, nodded with satisfaction.

Holding the envelope, he picked up the jewelry and eyed it appraisingly. He seemed to be fighting an inward battle with himself. And he was. A keen judge of jewels, he saw at a glance that there were thirty or forty thousand dollars' worth of diamonds, pearls and emeralds represented there. He knew a fence who, if handled properly, would grudgingly pay at least twenty thousand dollars for the lot. It was a powerful temptation to a man who had been going straight for two years.

And while he knelt there, fighting a silent and tense battle, a harsh voice snapped triumphantly: "Put up your hands!"

Jim Reilly hesitated the barest fraction of a second. Then slowly raised his hands, the brown manila envelope in his left fingers, the jewelry in his right.

"Stand up!"

Jim Reilly got to his feet, half turning to the source of that voice. And with an effort he suppressed a sharp exclamation. The figure who faced him might have been his twin. A tall, slender, scarlet-clad devil, tail dangling, cloth shoes marked with a cleft, scarlet mask leering, short stubby horns protruding out of the head. The other's hands were bare, his only difference from Jim Reilly. Flat, splayed fingers were gripping a blue-black automatic.

JIM REILLY had faced guns before, a sensation never pleasant. The small round dark hole in the muzzle of that automatic grew in size as he stared at it. Uneasily he shook off the thought of what would happen if that tight finger on the trigger should compress ever so slightly.

"Good evening, Mr. Dorrington," he greeted calmly.

A suspicious snort answered him. "So you know me. Who are you?"

Jim shrugged. "What does it matter? Quite a surprise seeing you here. Where have you been?"

"No business of yours!" Rodney Dorrington told him icily.

"None at all," Jim admitted cheerfully. "But your wife was wondering if you were out talking with Loretta Kincaid."

"Huh? Say, what do you know about her? Who are you, anyway?"

Jim shrugged again.

"Where is my wife?"

"I'm not her keeper."

"No!" Rodney Dorrington snapped. "You're not the keeper of anything! You're a crook! A damn thief! I don't know who you are, but I'm going to find out. I'm going to see which of my guests has the audacity to break into my desk, open my safe, steal my property. And then I'm going to turn you over to the law and prosecute you to the last inch. Understand?"

"Quite clearly," Jim agreed. "Can't we discuss this matter?"

Rodney Dorrington snorted.

Jim had known that would be the answer. He was sparring for time. He knew, perhaps better than Rodney Dorrington, exactly how bad a jam he was in. He had been caught cold, the evidence in his hands. That, coupled with his past record, was enough to assure a long prison stretch. How long, he did not like to think. Beef Miller would see that every factor was put in the blackest possible light.

Through the eyeholes of the mask he watched Rodney Dorrington warily. The automatic menacing him did not waver in the least. Any attempt at escape would be stopped with a blast of lead. And the man would be justified. No jury in the world would hold him accountable.

"Turn around!" Rodney Dorrington ordered harshly.

Jim weighed all the factors, and then slowly put his back to the man. He heard Dorrington's steps approach his back, felt the manila envelope snatched from his fingers.

"What have you got here?" Dorrington rasped suspiciously.

"I've been wondering," Jim murmured over his shoulder.

"Papers, eh? By heavens, the Blake letters! So you're interested in them, are you?"

"Why shouldn't I be interested in them?" Jim demurred.

"Drop that jewelry on the floor!"

The small fortune in emeralds, diamonds and pearls struck the carpet with a clinking thud. A hand scraped past his ear, yanked the mask down.

"Turn around!"

Jim did so, smiling slightly.

Rodney Dorrington studied his clean-cut features for a moment, taking in the high brow, the steady blue eyes, the aquiline nose, the thin, smiling mouth.

"I don't know you," he said with a puzzled note in his voice. "Never saw you before to my knowledge."

"No reason why you should," Jim sighed. "Our paths don't lie together. You're a big fruit importer, part owner of a steamship line, have your finger in half a dozen Central American republics, and a lot of dirt in this country. And I—" He broke off.

"And you?" Rodney Dorrington prompted grimly.

"And I am merely—"

"A thief!" Rodney Dorrington rasped. He flicked the manila envelope. "What's your interest in this?"

For a moment Jim Reilly's lean features went hard. More than that, contemptuous. "What's yours?" he countered.

Dorrington pulled his mask down, and for the first time the difference between them was clear. About the same build, their voices remarkably alike when muffled behind the masks, they were utterly unlike otherwise.

Rodney Dorrington's long hatchet face with its high-bridged hooked nose, its peering bright eyes beneath wispy eyebrows, its almost lipless, bloodless gash of a mouth, was a study in shrewdness, selfishness, slyness and cruelty.

Easy to believe some of the tales he had heard about this man. In poorer days Rodney Dorrington had fought the bush and hostile native factions of the Central American republics, while laying out by hook or crook great fruit plantations that were the foundation of his wealth and power. He had smashed roughshod over all opposition. It was whispered that the full measure of his nefarious and cruel dealings had never been known, and never would be. When it suited him he could be lavish with his money; or he could be utterly cruel, heartless and without mercy.

There was no mercy in his face now. The bloodless gash of a mouth was tight and drawn. The eyes were narrowed, gleaming with dislike; the stubby fingers cuddled the flat automatic as if the man yearned to use it.

Picking up the jewelry from the floor, Rodney Dorrington backed toward the door, rasping harshly: "Follow me! I'll take you downstairs and turn you over to the detectives on duty there. It'll be a diversion for my party." The ghost of an anticipatory smile widened his mouth. "And it will also show my guests what happens to anyone who violates my hospitality. It may stop anything more like this."

Jim did not answer him. His eyes were on the door toward which Dorrington was backing.

The knob was turning without a sound. The door opened a crack. Jim's eyes fastened on it with fascination. Someone was out there, someone interested in what was going on in this room. A premonition of trouble flashed through him. Something was going to happen.

And something did!

The door opened two inches, no more. A small round object thrust in an inch or so. There was a dull muffled pop.

Rodney Dorrington staggered a step forward. A look of intense surprise flashed over his face. His bloodless mouth gaped, turned up at the corners; his face contorted. The hand holding the flat automatic sagged down as if pulled by an invisible weight. A whistling gasp issued from his throat. He bowed forward, fell heavily to the floor, moved convulsively and lay still.

The small round object in the crack of the door shifted ever so slightly, covering Jim Reilly.

He recognized it for what it was— the silencer on the end of a revolver.

Someone standing outside the door had murdered Rodney Dorrington in cold blood! *And he was next.*

Jim dodged toward the corner of the room where he would be safe for a moment—too late. A second dull *pop* spat from the door. Jim felt a terrific blow over his heart. The world seemed to explode. He realized with a kind of queer wonder that he was falling and could not help himself. Hit over the heart—dying. Everything went black before his eyes.

Jim Reilly didn't know when he struck the floor and lay still—as Rodney Dorrington had done.

CHAPTER FOUR

"Little Hell Cat"

SHRILL feminine laughter in his ears, as Jim Reilly rolled over and groaned.

His eyes opened, blinked as the ceiling light struck hard into them. He sucked in a breath and a sharp stab of pain went through his chest. And memory came back.

Jim raised himself, saw that he was on the floor of the office. Everything was as he had last seen it. No—not exactly. A drift of papers was strewn over the floor around the desk.

A cool breeze blew against his face. The window was open. His eyes shifted to the door. There on the floor, sprawled face down, was the motionless body of Rodney Dorrington. A small pool of blood had collected around the head.

Out in the hall the shrill feminine laughter sounded again. Women chattering and giggling among themselves. That sound forced Jim to his feet in a hurry. He suddenly realized the danger of his position.

Murder had been done! He had not seen the killer, had no idea who it was —man or woman. He was in here with the dead body. And downstairs was Beef Miller, ready to slap any charge against him that seemed likely to hold.

What jury would believe his story? He had no business in the house. None that would hold water before the law. A thief, caught in the act, killing the man who found him. That was the story the law would get—and the story the law would believe. Jim Reilly saw it all clearly as he weaved unsteadily there in the middle of the floor.

Laughter again!

Suppose those women opened the door? His glance darted to the window. It was open now. It had been closed when he entered the room. He slipped to it, looked out. The sloping roof of the back porch confronted him. That way the killer had gone.

The voices in the hall receded. He breathed more easily. One danger gone for the moment. He went to the body. Rodney Dorrington was dead. No doubt about it. Shot square through the back of the head.

Jim's mind flashed back to that brief encounter outside. Murder had been mentioned then. And murder had been done. It came to him then that he had been subconsciously expecting it ever since he had been in the house. But he had never thought he would be entangled with it this way.

Who was the girl, he wondered. What was the mystery about her? If she had know there was danger of a killing why hadn't she said something to Rodney Dorrington? Or notified the police? What was she doing here apparently alone? Who was the person she had thought she was talking to?

And why had Rodney Dorrington been killed?

Those and many other questions pounded in his mind as he turned away from the body.

The desk had been looted, the safe rifled. The jewels that had been in Rodney Dorrington's hand were gone. The manila envelope was gone also. And every paper in the desk and safe seemed to have been gone over hastily, those unwanted tossed aside, others taken. He went to the safe. The large sum in bank notes was gone.

All that Jim got in brief seconds. He gave a thought to himself. His side was aching with every breath. He looked down over his heart for signs of blood. None there—and he had expected death.

He opened the scarlet suit, the clothes beneath, and looked at his bare chest. A great purplish swelling covered the heart. And he saw then what had saved his life.

The bullet had gone true, would have brought death quick and certain but for the case of steel tools that reposed over the heart. The bullet had smashed against the steel. The shock had knocked him unconscious. He found where the bullet had glanced out of the side of the case, grazed his chest and dropped down next to his skin. He was alive only by the grace of an accident.

Jim weighed the odds. Patsy Peters was down below waiting for him. He couldn't go out the window and leave Patsy. Downstairs he could still pass for Rodney Dorrington. He had been out only a quarter of an hour. Discovery that he was not Rodney Dorrington would have meant a search of the house before this.

No more voices in the hall. He opened the door cautiously and slipped out. And then almost bolted back in again as he saw the stocky figure of a Pierrot appear at the head of the stairs and start toward him. Even at that distance he recognized the iron-gray mustache of Beef Miller.

Muscles tightening, he weighed the matter. Had his disguise been penetrated? Was Miller looking for him? Should he wait and see—or bolt back through the open window?

And as he stood there undecided, Beef Miller called: "I say, Mr. Dorrington, I'd like to see you."

"Right," said Jim coolly, and making sure the door was closed he walked to meet the detective.

MILLER said as they met: "One of the servants reported to the butler that he thought he saw someone jump off the back-porch roof. I went out there and looked around. There were footprints on the grass where he landed, all right. And upstairs I saw a lighted window open. While I was standing there you looked out. Kind of puzzled me. Do you know anything about it? Everything all right?"

"Quite all right," Jim assured him.

"Don't often find people jumping off porch roofs at times like this," Miller commented; and it was hard to tell whether there was suspicion in his voice or not.

"It happened tonight," Jim replied. He managed a chuckle. "Friend of mine had a little too much to drink already. He bet me he could jump off the roof, and nothing I could say would stop him. He seemed sober enough to handle his feet, so I let him."

And he added as an afterthought, "Did the servant see what happened to him? I was expecting him to come back up."

"He went around the side of the house," Miller said. "I didn't see him come back in. Funny thing about it. The servant thought it might be you at the moment. He said he was sure the man who jumped had on a devil's suit like you're wearing."

The words tied one more knot in the chain of evidence. The Dutch milkmaid who talked with the soft Spanish accent had been looking for a man dressed like a devil. That man had come. She had either failed to see him or had been unable to stop him. He had come to kill—and he had killed!

Three devils—himself, Rodney Dorrington, and the stranger. And death for one of them. His mind whirled at the tangle of mystery and menace.

Miller stared at his hands. "Funny," he said. "Every time I see you your hands are different. One time you're wearin' gloves an' the next you're not."

"I expect part of the time you've been looking at my friend," said Jim calmly. "He had on a suit like this all right. Only he wasn't wearing gloves."

"Yes, he was," Miller insisted. "I saw him go up. He's a shorter man than you, you know. Not a chance of him being mistaken for you."

"Er—that's right," Jim assented hastily.

Once more the cold sweat was coming out on his forehead. Why didn't the fool get downstairs? If he kept this up he was going to stumble on something in spite of himself.

Beef Miller's eyes were on his hands. "Funny you didn't remember that your friend had on gloves," he remarked. "And your hands are funny, too. When the gloves are off they look short and stubby, and when they're on, they look long and slender."

"You watch close, don't you?"

And as Jim said that he grew more tense, if possible. For in the hall ahead of them a door opened. He heard voices. A young woman costumed as an Indian princess stepped across the hall—and entered the bedroom that belonged to Rodney Dorrington's wife!

And in that moment Jim realized that discovery was close. Miller was speaking, but he hardly heard what the man was saying.

"Eh, I beg pardon?" he said. "I didn't understand you."

"I said we notice little things like hands," Miller stated sociably. "Things like that are tricks of the trade, you know. Never get far if we only went by photographs. But I never noticed how much gloves changed hands like they do yours. I wonder if you'd take 'em off an' put 'em back on so I can see for myself. Never know when it'll come in handy."

Was Beef Miller toying with him as a cat would with a mouse? Did he suspect the truth already? Jim did the only thing possible. He didn't dare let Miller look at his bare hands. His camera eye would see they were not the stubby hands of Dorrington he had noticed.

"Sorry," he said curtly. "I have wasted too much time up here already. I must get down to my guests. Come along."

Miller made no protest, came along with him, chatting sociably. They descended the stairs. And as the hall below came into sight Jim cursed silently to himself.

Standing in the arch of the doorway, where she could watch the stairs, was the Dutch milkmaid.

Her eyes were on him as he came down the stairs beside Miller. Jim could feel their intent stare through the eyeholes of her mask. And that same mask hid the expression on her face.

What was she going to do, he wondered. Denounce him here? Blurt out her suspicions?

The merriment was at its height. The dance floor in the next room was crowded. People were moving in and out. Patsy Peters was not in sight.

She stepped forward and confronted him. "I want to speak to you," she said.

"I'm busy right now," Jim answered gruffly. "A few minutes later if you don't mind."

Out of the corner of his eye he saw Beef Miller staring down at the scarlet-gloved hands. Only by an effort did he suppress the desire to thrust them behind his body.

And with startling suddenness a shrill scream sounded upstairs. A scream of fright and terror from a woman's throat.

"Murder! Help! Come quick!"

THOSE ghastly high-pitched cries of fright and terror struck everyone in the hall dumb and motionless for a moment.

There are times when the instinct to break and run comes to everyone. Such an impulse gripped Jim Reilly as he stood there rigid beside Beef Miller, the detective. He had no wish to face a death sentence—and it was reaching out for him with hideous certainty now. Death, for something he had not done!

The eyes of the Dutch milkmaid were staring at this masked face. Staring accusingly. In those split seconds of sudden silence Jim waited for her to cry out for his arrest.

Beef Miller uttered a startled exclamation. "What's happened?" he burst out.

"Call the police! He's dead!" was screamed again.

Beef Miller whirled to the stairs, snapping at Jim: "Come up! Something's happened!" And without waiting to see whether he was followed, Miller raced upstairs.

Jim whipped through the archway into the big room where the guests were dancing. The music and sound in there drowned the cries from above. Only those by the doorway had stopped, were staring questioningly. Jim plunged through them, peering about the room for Patsy Peters.

There he was near the back, standing against the wall!

Jim surged across the dance floor, politeness forgotten, ignoring those he bumped into. Patsy saw him coming, waited inquiringly. Jim caught his arm.

"Quick! Out of here!" he ordered Patsy. "The back way! Don't stop!"

And before the last word crossed his lips, Jim was striding toward the rear exit door with Patsy hurrying after him. No one stopped them. They got through the door, across the small hall, through the dining room and butler's pantry into the kitchen.

There all work had stopped. Philippe, the chef, and his assistants were huddled in dumb uneasiness.

"Monsieur!" Philippe cried at sight of the devil and imp bursting in on them. "Is there something wrong? We hear the screams upstairs! Screams of murder!"

"There is trouble!" Jim rapped back. "Stay here in the kitchen! The police are attending to everything!"

"What is it?" Suzette, the pretty maid, cried.

"Someone is dead!"

Jim was at the back door as he spoke. He cast a last look at them and spoke sternly: "Stay here in the kitchen, every one of you!" And then he strode across the back porch and out into the open night, leaving the kitchen staff gaping after him.

The lighted window on the second floor was still open. Excited voices drifted out.

"I hope those servants keep quiet for a few minutes!" Jim exclaimed to Patsy trotting beside him.

"What happened?" Patsy burted out.

"Murder!"

"Huh?"

"Murder! Rodney Dorrington was killed! Shot in the back of the head with a silencer! Almost got me, too!"

"Cripes!" Patsy gasped. "Then that dame was right after all. There was a killing laid out."

"It looks that way," Jim answered grimly. "And I'm on the spot for it. We both are, Patsy. You as an accessory. Beef Miller thought I was Dorrington. He knows different now. He'll be after us quick! He may be coming now!"

"An' we ain't got a chance," Patsy panted. "I told you we ought to bring a gat along, in case we got in a jam."

"Worst thing in the world. We might be tempted to use it."

"Hell—that's better than takin' a rap for murder!"

They were running across the lawn as they talked. They burst into the circle of light under the Japanese lanterns strung around the automobile parking space. The way was clear behind the long black roadster.

Jim slid in behind the wheel. Patsy tore open the door on the other side and plopped down on the seat. Jim stamped the starter, snapping on the ignition switch and snatching for the choke.

And as the motor caught with a rush, a slender figure stepped on the running board beside Jim. He felt the hard poke of a gun barrel in his side. It was the demure Dutch milkmaid with the long thick yellow braids. She asked icily: "Where are you going?"

"Wh-where did you come from?" Jim stammered in surprise, staring at her.

"I thought you would slip out the back way," she retorted. "So I walked out the front and kept an eye on your car here."

THERE was no weakness or hesitation about that gun in his side. She knew exactly what she was doing. Patsy was leaning forward, staring intently at them.

"Don't try to get away," the girl warned him coldly.

"Do I look like it?" Patsy snarled at her.

"What are you going to do?" Jim panted, sitting rigid while the motor idled.

His glance strayed for a moment toward the house. Each instant he expected the pursuit to burst out after them.

"I warned you there was to be no killing here tonight," the girl reminded coldly.

"I didn't do any killing!" Jim snapped.

"No?" There was unbelief in her voice. "Who did then?"

"I don't know."

"You lie! I saw you go upstairs! You killed Dorrington after all, Daly."

"Don't stand there talking!" Jim begged. "We've got to get away from here! I didn't kill the man, but I can't prove that I didn't. Put that gun away and listen to reason!"

"Listen to lies, you mean!" the girl told him contemptuously. "I've heard enough of them to last me a long time. And I'm through. I'm going to act now!"

"What are you going to do?"

"Take you back and turn you over to the police."

"Don't try that," Jim warned.

"Get out of the car," was her unyielding answer.

While they had been talking, Jim had cast ahead to this result, and set himself for it. His left arm snapped back from the wheel in an unexpected lightning-like motion. The elbow knocked the gun away from his side.

It exploded at his back, driving the bullet through the leather seat covering. He had been right. She was ready to shoot to back up her words.

That knowledge whipped Jim around in the seat with superhuman quickness. His right hand caught her gun arm, his left clamped around the wrist. A hard twist brought the gun up, pointing back away from him. So hard that the muzzle jammed through the fabric of the top.

"Drop it!" Jim gritted.

But she held on to the weapon stubbornly. He didn't want to risk breaking her arm; didn't dare release it for fear she would shoot again. Patsy solved the matter. He had leaped up from his seat at the sound of the shot. Now he threw himself across Jim and caught the gun. A wrench—a gasp from behind the girl's mask, and Patsy had the weapon.

"Throw her out an' let's get going!" Patsy panted, dropping back in his place. And he added angrily: "The little hell cat!"

It had all happened so quickly the shot had been the only sound. She had not screamed. An idea came to Jim as he held her there. This girl was the only link he had with the killer. She knew the story behind it. She could probably put him on the trail of that third scarlet-clad figure who had come with murder in his heart.

He had to find that man to clear himself and Patsy. And he wanted the man for another reason. The manila envelope was gone. He must have it and the money and jewels also. Until they were returned the guilt of their theft was on him.

With his right hand he snapped the door catch, kicked it open against her and twisted out. She struck at his face, tearing the mask away. The soft light from the gaudy lanterns overhead fell full on his features.

A gasp came from behind her mask. "Who are you?" she cried.

"Doesn't matter now!" Jim grunted, whirling her around and shoving her into the car. "I don't know you. Never saw you before. Haven't any idea what this is all about. But you have. This killing's blamed on me. I'm going to find out who did it. And you're going to help me!"

She was struggling against him, trying to keep out of the car. "Stop!" she gasped. "I'm all mixed up! I want to talk to you about it——here!"

"No time. They'll be coming after us. Get in there!"

Again Patsy came to the rescue. He caught her around the middle and hauled her in the car, warning: "Don't make no noise, sister, or you'll get hurt!"

Suddenly she yielded, sank into the seat beside Patsy, breathing hard.

CHAPTER FIVE

Trapped!

JIM slipped behind the wheel once more, slammed the door, backed the car out with a rush. And he wasn't sure as they shot down the driveway that a cry didn't come from the front of the house. Their escape had been seen.

He took the turn into the street in screaming second gear, tires shrieking as they skidded on the macadam.

The Venetian Way across Biscayne Bay was the nearest route to Miami. Jim did just the opposite of what nine out of ten persons would have done. He drove east into Miami Beach, zigzagging through the streets to lose possible pursuit, and turned north. Shortly they were speeding along the little-traveled, lonesome boulevard that paralleled the beach.

The bright lights of a car approached and passed them, leaving the dark ribbon of asphalt stretching ahead. A hundred yards to the right lay the restless gleam of the open Atlantic, and now and then the white frothy wash of surf on the sand was visible. An occasional palm stood dark and stiff. The cool night air whipped in around them as the roadster whined up toward sixty.

The girl had sat silent since starting, now and then turning her head and staring at Jim's face. Jim risked a glance at her, was baffled by the mask hiding her face. He reached over and pulled it away. She did not protest.

The faint light of the instrument panel, shone on determined, even features, slightly oval in contour. A rather pretty girl—one in ten. Black eyebrows over dark brooding eyes, cheekbones slightly high, a small perfectly shaped nose, a grave unsmiling mouth with lips rouged heavily.

Speaking loudly so as to be heard above the rush of wind, Jim said: "Take off that wig."

Gravely she raised her hands and lifted off the winged cap and the wig of yellow hair. Beneath it her own hair, sloe-black and soft, framed her head in soft waves.

It was astonishing. Another woman was revealed. Gone the suggestion of Dutch stolidity; and in its place a flashing vital girl of the South. One glance, even if one had not heard her softly accented speech, was enough to tell that the blood of Castile ran in her veins.

"What is your name?" Jim asked.

She shrugged, did not answer.

"You may as well tell it. We have to call you something."

She looked at him gravely. He had the feeling that he was being weighed, estimated. She showed no evidence of fear. Rather weariness—on her guard every moment. And Jim realized then that this girl was going to be hard to deal with—unless she willed it otherwise herself.

"You may call me Juanita," she said after a moment; and in the words was a trace of royal assent, as if she were conferring a great favor on them.

"What's the rest of your name?"

Another shrug. "That is all you need know."

And after a moment she asked in turn: "Where are you taking me?"

Jim answered truthfully, "I don't know just yet. That depends on you."

"What do you mean?"

"Just what I said."

He slowed down a little. They were approaching Seventy-ninth Street. "Who did you think I was when you spoke to me this evening?" he questioned.

She did not answer. He tried again. "Whom were you expecting to come to that house tonight and commit murder?"

No answer again. Her red lips pressed together in a tight line as if she were steeling herself against his questions.

"You were talking about the police," Jim pressed. "They'll be interested to know why you didn't report your suspicions. It makes you an accessory after the murder. You knew Dorrington was going to be killed, and you didn't raise a hand to stop it."

"I—I wasn't sure." It was wrung from her under the stress of strong emotion.

The street light, the little cluster of houses at Seventy-ninth Street rushed at them. Jim slowed the car more, made the turn west toward Biscayne Bay, and then asked sharply: "Why weren't you sure?"

"I—please don't ask me questions!"

"You didn't want Dorrington killed?"

"No."

"He was."

"I know that," she answered wretchedly.

"And an innocent man is being blamed for the murder," Jim reminded.

"You are guilty of something or you wouldn't have run away as you did," she flashed. "Why didn't you tell me I was speaking to the wrong person tonight?"

"I wanted to see what you were going to do," Jim confessed. "I thought at first you were kidding me. Any sane person would have expected you to go to the police at once."

"I know," she agreed heavily. "I was at fault. But I thought I had warned the right man. I did not think he would dare go ahead after he knew I was present watching him, ready to turn him over to the police if he disregarded my warning."

"And you didn't see the other man?"

"No. I—I thought you were he. I was watching you."

"He was dressed in a suit like I am wearing," Jim told her.

"Yes. That was the plan," she assented.

THEY had crossed the bridge over the east channel now and were running across the long lighted causeway that sprawled from the island of Miami Beach to the city on the mainland. The causeway was deserted. Jim pulled over to the side of the road and stopped the car abruptly.

"Out of these suits, Patsy," he snapped.

It was the work of seconds to leap out of the car, jerk the costumes off, ball them up and throw them into the water. They reentered the car clad in conservative suits to which passing eyes would give no second look.

And as Jim sent the roadster tooling forward swifty, he said to the mysterious Juanita between them: "A large sum of money, some valuable jewelry and papers were taken. Among them were some papers that I want badly. All that in addition to the murder charge I'm running away from. You see why you've got to tell me what you know before I let you go."

"Papers?" she exclaimed.

"Yes."

Jim sensed her foot tapping the floor impatiently. A frown of worried indecision etched little lines between her eyes. She spoke abruptly, as if her mind had suddenly been made up. "Tell me what happened upstairs."

Jim did, cautiously omitting the part he had played in rifling the safe.

"I see," Juanita nodded when he finished. "He must have slipped upstairs when I was not looking. And after he had killed Dorrington he escaped through the window and never came back in the house."

"Something like that," Jim agreed.

She hesitated, then said clearly: "I will help you. For those papers that he took must be destroyed. I must have them and burn them myself."

"Why?" Jim asked bluntly.

"They are dangerous. I—I'm afraid they will cause death to one who—who is very dear to me."

"I see," Jim said understandingly. And then he went on briskly. "It's a bargain. Those papers to you—my papers to me. The money and jewels back to Dorrington's wife—and the killer, if we get him, to the police."

A small hand met his at the rim of the steering wheel. They shook hands on the matter silently.

Jim asked, "Have you a gun?"

"I have," Patsy said significantly.

"Yours. And I'll use it if I have to."

"You may have to," she told him gravely.

"That's what I'm thinking," Patsy replied sourly. And he spoke across her to Jim, as if she was not there. "Watch out for a trap, Jim. You can't tell what we're gettin' into."

No protest of indignation came from Juanita. She had grown thoughtful.

"No, we cannot tell what we are getting into," she agreed. "But of one thing I am sure, my friends. Very sure."

"What's that?" Patsy queried suspiciously.

"If they find out what we know and what we want, they will kill us quick. You understand? Quick!"

The smell of rotted vegetation, of black water and stagnant mudbanks crept around the black roadster as it slowly crushed a way through crackling palmetto scrub and came to a stop.

The headlights were off, had been that way since the machine turned from the highway into the narrow sandy road, and presently off that into the screening palmettos and pines at one side.

Juanita stirred on the seat and said in a low voice: "We walk from here."

They got out of the car. Patsy muttered in a troubled voice: "I don't like this, Jim. No telling what we're walkin' into."

"You do not trust me?" Juanita asked angrily in the darkness that enveloped them.

"No more'n a slick dime," Patsy assured her. "An' don't forget, sister— I'm packin' your gun. I'll use it if we poke into anything funny."

"Loosen up, Patsy," Jim advised tolerantly.

More and more he had been feeling a measure of sympathy for this girl since she had promised to help them.

True, little more than directions had passed her lips. But as she had ridden in silence beside him, Jim had seemed that she was in the grip of strong emotion. His doubts had changed to conviction that she was with them, trying to help them.

Her directions had been curt, clear, taking them south through Miami into the open country, with a brief stop at the hotel for Jim's revolver. Miles out of the city she had ordered the headlights off and the roadster into the small side road that led toward the sea.

THE country around was desolate, silent, lonely. The Everglades were near, beyond them the tangled wilderness of marsh and swamp, of water-bound cypress, trailing creepers and festooned Spanish moss. It was the dank smell of all that which drifted past them on the off-shore breeze.

Patsy grumbled something and fell silent as the girl led them back to the road and on toward the sea. Patsy's silence was as much of a protest as his words had been.

A quarter of a mile dropped behind, perhaps more. Their feet scuffed softly on the sandy track. The palmettos rustled in ghastly fashion. Now and then a small animal fled away from their presence.

And then a light appeared ahead, winking briefly for a moment before it vanished. A light in the air, above the ground.

"What's that?" Jim husked to Juanita.

"The house."

He felt her hand on his arm, soft, firm, reassuring as she guided him ahead. And a few moments later the house took shape. A two-storied residence, square, angular, brooding darkly in the night.

The top rim of a silver moon was creeping up in the east. Its first ray shimmered on the open sea beyond the house.

A thread of light on the second floor marked the spot where the light had appeared briefly. Jim's hand slipped in his pocket and cuddled the butt of the revolver. "D'you think our man's in there?" he whispered.

"Yes. And two or three more. Watch them, my friend."

"We'll handle them," Jim promised under his breath. "What's the best way to get inside?"

"There is a side door, probably unlocked."

No sign of life was visible as they slipped silently across a lawn toward the north side of the house. The track led there. The dark shape of an automobile became visible before a stucco garage off at one side. Jim wondered if it had brought the killer from Rodney Dorrington's house on Palm Island. He did not ask. They were not speaking now as they moved quietly toward the side of the house—three dark shadows.

Shrubbery grew here at the north side of the house, large luxurious bushes sweeping to the height of a man's head, all but hiding the small side portico and door. But Juanita was familiar with the place. She led them unerringly to the door.

Shoes barely scraped on the flagstone steps and small square terrace as she stepped to the screen door and pulled it out softly. Jim and Patsy crowded close, ready to enter after her.

And in that instant the quiet night erupted unexpectedly. There was a rush out of the bushes on either side. Dark forms swarmed on them.

A terrific blow struck the side of Jim's head. A leaping figure lunged into him. He staggered, trying to jerk the revolver out of his pocket. It caught in the lining. A hand grabbed his arm. A gun barrel jabbed painfully in his back. And a threatening voice cried in his ear: "I weel shoot!"

Patsy, fighting someone on the other side and swearing loudly, bumped into him. A pistol exploded with a roar. A cry of pain followed—then a groan. Patsy staggered into him again and slumped suddenly down over his feet.

That shot, that cry and Patsy's collapse drove Jim berserk. No matter that a gun was against his back, that further resistance might send a shot tearing into his body. He whirled, striking savagely at the figure standing behind him.

No sane man would have done it. The very unexpectedness saved his life. The pistol spat fire and lead. He felt the concussion of hot gases bite into his coat as the bullet missed and his fist smashed into the side of the stranger's jaw with every ounce of his strength behind it.

The dark figure that had menaced him catapulted off the steps and dropped to hands and knees on the grass. There were others. Jim swung around to meet them—and stumbled over Patsy's inert form. He struck a second figure, wrapped his arms around its waist to pull himself up.

And a pistol barrel swung hard against the top of his head. Tiny points of light flashed through the darkness; strength ran from his muscles like spilled water. A second blow beat him down to his knees, where he swayed in a drunken stupor, helpless. Hands seized him, jerked him to his feet, caught his arms behind him and frisked him quickly, taking the gun out of his pocket.

Dimly he heard an angry stream of Spanish erupt behind him, sensed a rush from the man he had knocked down,

felt dully the impact of a blow on the side of his head.

Jim shook his head weakly, ignoring the pain, trying to clear his senses.

Dully he heard Juanita cry: "Hold them! They will get away!"

And a voice answered between heavy breaths: "You! What are you doing here?"

A silvery laugh greeted that question. Juanita replied gaily: "I brought them here to you. They are dangerous. They know too much."

"Who are they?"

"I don't know. But Rodney Dorrington has been killed, and one of them was in the room at the time. They are looking for the man who killed him."

An oath of surprise met her statement. "Are they from the police?"

"Perhaps," Juanita said carelessly. "You can make them talk. I have done my part. I brought them here. They were so simple and trusting. I could hardly keep from laughing at them."

She laughed then, amused, scornful.

That mirth did more than anything else to drive the fog from Jim's senses. Hot anger coursed through him. Anger at himself. The girl had been leading them into a trap from the moment her opposition had vanished.

Looking back he could see it now. Her wits had conquered where her strength was not equal. A clever actress with her talk about helping one dear to her. He had been a fool. A sentimental fool to trust her for a moment.

Patsy had been right after all!

CHAPTER SIX

The Mysterious Stranger

THE sound of a speeding automobile engine came to them. The bright shaft of a pair of headlights silvered the lawn beside the house.

"Who is that?" Juanita asked sharply.

Jim could see four men grouped about them, two holding him. The girl who had betrayed them was standing in the doorway, the white cloth of her costume standing out against the door. One of the men beside him answered gruffly in the same strong accent that had been spoken before: "We soon see."

And they did. The automobile swung around the corner of the house and slid to a stop. The door on the other side swung open. A man jumped out. His voice cracked at them: "Who is it?"

"Ees that you, Daly?"

"Yeah!" came the crisp answer. "What's the matter here?"

"Eet ees all right. We have visitors."

"Who?" the stranger asked as he came around the front of the car. A flashlight in his hand sprayed light over them. A startled exclamation came from the stranger.

"Say, who's the lady? I've seen that outfit tonight."

"She ees Senorita Alvarez," the spokesman of the four stated. "She was at Dorrington's tonight."

"Yeah. An' what was she doing there?" Daly snapped. There was wariness in his voice.

"That," said the same speaker, "I do not know yet. But she brought these two men here. She says they are dangerous."

The light flashed full in Jim's face.

"Christ!"

There was anger and fear in the startled exclamation that burst from the stranger. He stepped close to Jim, played the light full in his face. Slowly it traveled down, halted over Jim's heart. A sharp suck of breath was audible.

Looking down, Jim saw the small hole in the front of his coat, where the bullet that almost cost him his life had penetrated. And Jim realized then that he was facing the killer of Rodney Dorrington, the man who had shot at him in cold blood, and probably had thought him dead until this moment. The third of the three scarlet-clad devils. The killer whose guilt had been thrust on him.

Patsy stirred at their feet, where he had been allowed to lie. Stirred and groaned. And was for the moment ignored.

"What's he doing here?" Daly demanded thickly. "Quick, Romero, spill it!"

"Senorita Alvarez brought him."

"What for?"

And the girl explained calmly: "They wanted the killer of Rodney Dorrington, my friend. They said they were going to find him. And so I brought them here——" she laughed again——"where they could find him, and we would have them safe."

"You? Why you? Where do you come in on this?"

"She is Don Alvarado Alvarez' daughter," Romero explained smoothly. "He has been one of us. It is natural she do what she can to help. So she bring them here and they walk like rabbits into the trap."

"Huh. Pretty smart dame," Daly grunted.

"You have done what was agreed?"

"Yeah," Daly grunted briefly. "An' I cleaned his desk for you. Stuff's in the car."

"Get it."

"All right. Take those two in. I want to look at 'em."

Daly returned to the car. Patsy had stirred again, tried drunkenly to sit up, groaning slightly.

"Patsy, how are you?" Jim demanded.

The other two men jerked Patsy to his feet, held him upright.

Patsy swore at them, answered Jim with more life. "My blasted head feels like it's busted open."

"Aren't you shot?"

"Hell, no," Patsy replied. "If I am I don't know it. I tried to get one of them, an' just before I cracked down with the gat something slammed me on the head. That's all I knew until I heard you talkin' over me. Did I miss the dirty highbinder?"

"Sí, senor," Romero said drily. "Eet was me."

"Too bad," Patsy said glumly. "How about the dame?"

And Juanita Alvarez uttered a silvery laugh. "It was so easy, little man."

"I was lookin' for it," Patsy stated sourly. "You dirty, double-crossin' little spitfire! If I ever get a chance at you again I'm gonna crack you first an' talk afterwards. Women always was poison to me, an' I had a hunch you were double strength. I told you, Jim."

"Sorry," Jim agreed. "My fault. I'll know better next time too."

Daly rejoined them. "Let's go in," he urged impatiently.

JUANITA opened the door, stepped inside. Jim and Patsy were hustled after her by the men who held them and Daly brought up the rear. They went through a dark hall, stepped into a room. A switch clicked inside the door, lights flashed on, revealing a big sparsely furnished room. For the first time Jim got a good look at the lot of them.

Romero was a short, stocky man, wide-jowled and olive-skinned. He had the marks of strength and breeding about him. Even now Jim felt he might have liked the fellow in different circumstances.

The man on his other side was tall and swarthy, coarse-featured and lowering. Both the men who held Patsy's arms were short, dark also. One was dapper; one squat, coarse-featured, suggesting a heavy admixture of Indian blood.

Daly was Anglo Saxon. One glance showed that. Dead white skin, black eyebrows, a thin nose, a tight mouth, and the shifty predatory manner of the big city slums. Jim placed him at a glance. A crook on the make—unscrupulous, deadly. The puzzle was how he had become mixed up with these other people.

Daly stepped in front of Jim, jerked open his coat and shirt. "You're the guy who was in the room with Dorrington," he said out of the corner of his mouth. "I dropped you clean. No fakin' about that. An' how the hell you turn up here is beyond me. Oh—I see."

He had found the instrument case that had deflected the bullet. And his eyes widened as he took it out and saw the contents. An oath of astonishment burst from him. "Look what this mug's packin' around!" he rasped. "A regular cannon's pack! An' high-class stuff too!"

"I do not understand," Romero said, frowning. "What ees cannon pack?"

"Tools. These things," Daly told him, showing the case of tools. Suddenly Daly laughed harshly. "I get it now," he said. "The safe was open when I crashed the study. He was makin' a play there himself an' got cut off by Dorrington before I showed up. Ain't that right, mug?"

"Wise guy," Jim agreed. "Now that we understand each other, suppose you tell these fellows we're good people and let us go."

Daly scowled. "Like hell! You know too much. Maybe I'm wrong. You may be a couple of dicks for all I know. I guess you are, or you wouldn't give a damn who knocked off Dorrington. Wanted to follow me, did you? Well, you're here. Now like it."

The short, swarthy man holding Patsy's elbow with one hand and an automatic ready with the other, directed a stream of Spanish at Romero. And Romero said gloomily to Daly: "What we do with them?"

"Knock 'em off," Daly said without emotion. "They know too much. I've done my part. There's the stuff outa his desk you wanted." He gestured toward a packed linen sack he had dropped inside the door. "Now I want my jack an' good sleep nights with them outa the way. You go up for murder if they put one over on you."

A swift interchange of Spanish broke out among the four. Their faces darkened and the glances cast at Jim and Patsy were threatening.

The Senorita Alvarez had been watching in silence. Now she stepped up to Jim and snapped her fingers in his face. "My friend, it looks bad for you," she mocked. "I am sorry. see—I weep." She laughed.

Romero and the others grinned.

Jim stared at her steadily. Ever since he had learned she had tricked them he had been puzzling over her. She was an enigma, a mystery. He found it impossible to reconcile her attempt to stop the killing at Dorrington's and her threat to turn Patsy and himself over to the police, with her subsequent actions.

"Sanchez," said Romero sharply, and spoke in Spanish.

Jim went alert at the name Senorita Alvarez had used at their first meeting. The swarthy little man beside Patsy handed his gun to his companion and

left the room hurriedly. He was quickly back with light strong rope.

They tied Patsy's arms behind him lashed his knees so he could barely walk; and then did the same to Jim And there was nothing to do but submit.

"Lock them up," Romero ordered "After I look the papers over we will attend to them."

"And what is it you do?" Senorita Alvarez queried with a smile. "Kill them?"

"Sí, we will have to kill them," Romero said regretfully. "It is war."

"War, is it?" Patsy raved as the door slammed behind them and he hobbled across the bare little room and dropped on the narrow cot that stood against the wall. "If it's war I'm a duchess! It sounds more like butchery. Jim, we're in a hell of a mess."

"With devils all tangled up in it," Jim agreed with a twisted grin.

Patsy scowled. "Never mind the wisecrackin'. Those guys mean business. They're gonna knock us off tonight."

"They seem to figure on something like that," Jim agreed. And he added: "I'd walk five miles for a cigarette right now. And not a chance of getting at the pack in my pocket while I'm roped this way."

PATSY leaned forward on the edge of the cot, brooding. "Every time I think of that dame I see red," he grated. "She sure took us for a couple of suckers right."

"Me, you mean," Jim corrected.

Patsy said nothing.

They had been hustled up a flight of stairs to the second floor of the house, then up a narrow stair well to this bare little room in the attic. Nothing in it but the cot, a plain chair and a washstand. The ceiling slanted low over their heads. There was one small window.

Jim hobbled awkwardly over to that window, found that it was nailed shut. And Patsy spoke the thought in his mind. "Even if we busted the glass, there's no one around to hear us."

The door had been locked after them. A guard had been left outside. They heard him clear his throat, strike a match. The law wanted them for murder. The men downstairs were plainly going to stop their tongues. A sordid ending to a dizzy, hectic evening.

Jim edged nearer Patsy, spoke under his breath soberly. "Patsy, do we take it like a couple of tied roosters, or do we flap our wings and scrap?"

"How are we gonna scrap like this?" Patsy demanded.

Jim grinned crookedly. "Stand up an' turn around."

Patsy did that. Jim backed up to him. His hands and wrists were bound tightly. Already the blood was slowing down, numbness stealing through the muscles. But he could still move the end of his fingers awkwardly.

Those fingers felt the cords at Patsy's wrists, located the knot. It had been jerked tight; too tight for his cramped, numbed fingers. But he plucked patiently with the skill, the sureness of touch he had used on the knurled safe knob.

One knot yielded. Then another. The cords loosened about Patsy's wrists, dropped free.

"Hurry!" Patsy breathed.

Jim was already working on the cords holding Patsy's elbows. They were both strained, tense. They could hear the man stirring about outside, knew that he might open the door any instant, discover what they were doing and stop it.

Jim talked as he worked in an effort to lull the guard's suspicions.

The elbow cords yielded finally to Jim's patient plucking. Patsy stripped the ropes away, hurled them to the floor, sat down on the cot and attacked the cords about his knees. Then went to work hurriedly on Jim. A few minutes later they faced each other with grins of satisfaction.

"Now," said Jim softly, "watch the fireworks."

Swinging his arms briskly to start the circulation he stepped softly to the chair and set it over beside the door. Then he whispered in Patsy's ear. Patsy nodded, dragged the cot noisily toward the window. Next he pulled the washstand out from the wall. A key turned in the lock. The door opened hurriedly. The short, scowling figure of Sanchez stepped into the room, automatic in hand. Patsy ducked down behind the washstand.

Jim had been pressed flat against the wall with the chair poised over his head. He smashed it down on Sanchez' head. The hard edge of the heavy seat did the work. Sanchez dropped dumbly, without firing the automatic. Jim discarded the chair, was on him like a cat. He straightened up with the gun in his hand.

"What a smack!" Patsy breathed, dodging out from behind the washstand and joining him. "Kill him?"

"Probably not," Jim grunted, dragging the limp form into the room. "Come on, we've got to work fast."

THEY left Sanchez in possession of the room, closed the door, locked it and took the key. The attic was divided into four rooms and a narrow hall with a window at one end and the stair well at the other. A small light bulb in the ceiling gave dim illumination.

Jim went to the window. It was

nailed shut. Looking out he could see the ground far below. A sheer drop, dangerous. Turning back he husked to Patsy: "Guess we'll have to go down the stairs. Probably break a leg if we smash the glass and drop."

A groan cut off any answer Patsy might have made. They stopped, listening. The groan came again, apparently from behind a door at their elbow.

There was a key in the lock. Jim turned it, opened the door. The room was dark. Enough light entered to show a drop cord hanging from the ceiling. Something stirred, breathed hoarsely. Gun ready for instant use, Jim edged to the cord, turned on the light. And the sight that met their eyes held them in gaping astonishment for a moment.

The room was little different from the one they had left. On the cot against the left wall lay the bound and gagged figure of an elderly man. He was trussed so tightly movement was virtually impossible. His eyes blinked in the sudden light, widened at sight of them. He groaned weakly behind the gag again.

"Poor devil," Patsy muttered. "What are those rats downstairs runnin', a jail?"

Jim slipped the gun in his pocket, stooped over the cot and removed the gag.

"Thank you!" the old man whispered weakly.

His tousled hair was gray, his thin face hawk-like and imperious. Drawn now with emotion and shock.

Jim quickly unfastened the ropes, helped the stranger to sit up. But as soon as his supporting arm was taken away the spare form sagged back again.

"Tight ropes cut off blood!" the other gasped. "Brought on heart attack! I—I will lie here."

He spoke fluent English, but it w accented. Spanish, too, by the loo of him.

"We can't stay around here a night," Patsy warned.

"Buck up," Jim smiled down at th stranger. "I think we'll get you out o this. And then you can tell all abou it. No time to talk now."

He and Patsy left the room.

"They're bad eggs," Jim muttered.

"We'll crack 'em!" Patsy uttered grimly. "And that dame—"

They reached the dark stair well slipped down it silently. Jim opened the door at the bottom an inch or so and peered out into the second-floor hall. It was lighted. The harsh murmur of voices became audible downstairs on th first floor.

Jim opened the door wider and glided into the hall, Patsy after him. Several yards away was the top of the stairs, a small alcove and a feminine figure standing there, her back to them.

Patsy sucked in his breath a t the sight. It was Senorita Alvarez, a telephone in her hand, receiver to her ear. She was speaking so low that the tones barely reached them. Up the stairs drifted the sounds of other voices. Jim recognized the rasping tones of Daly, the harder accent of Romero and his companions.

This encounter was another bit of bad luck. If the girl saw them she would scream, warn the others. A turn of her head would betray them. One step on a squeaky board might. She started to hang up the receiver.

Jim risked everything in a swift silent rush to her side. She sensed his presence just before he reached her, started to turn. And Jim seized her, clapping his hand over her mouth, stifling her exclamation of fear. She struggled. Her hand struck the telephone, knocking it crashing to the floor. And in that in-stent she saw who held her. She stopped struggling.

"Keep quiet!" Jim whispered fiercely.

To his amazement he saw a smile break over her face. It seemed to be relief.

Downstairs the voices had stopped. A chair scraped. Then Alvarez called loudly: "W'at was that?"

CHAPTER SEVEN

Devil's Due

JIM pulled the girl back toward the shelter of the hall, keeping his hand over her mouth. For a second they were visible at the top of the stairs—and in that moment Daly rushed out of the room below, gun in hand.

One look up was enough. His revolver jerked high, barked loudly in the confined space, disregarding the girl close to Jim. The man was a crack shot, or cursed with luck. A hammer blow struck Jim in the shoulder, whirling him off balance. The arm holding the girl went limp, numb as he staggered back. The automatic fell from his fingers. She twisted free.

"Watch out!" Patsy shouted warningly.

It came too late. She snatched the gun off the floor.

Jim felt himself wondering if she was going to finish what Daly had almost done. And then he got the greatest shock of the evening. For instead of whirling and covering him with the gun, she fired down the stairs at Daly. It was another quick sharp scene, over in seconds. Daly's revolver spat loudly and he dived back into the room out of sight.

Bits of plaster were still drifting down from the ceiling where Daly's last shot had struck as Senorita Alvarez

pushed Jim back from the stairs and shoved the revolver at Patsy.

"Take it!" she gasped. "They'll be out again!" And she faced Jim and begged: "Where did he hit you?"

Patsy looked as near stunned as a man could as he cradled the automatic pistol in his hand. His eyes shifted between the stairs and the girl, as if he could not quite decide what to do.

"Got me in the shoulder, I think," Jim declared, feeling the spot.

Already the coat was wet with blood around the spot; the arm itself felt numb, useless. Jim's blood-stained fingers lingered there as he stared at her. And her eyes met his, wide with concern—and something more.

"Am I cuckoo, or are you?" Patsy's voice cracked dazedly at her. "Did you gimme this gat or did I dream it?"

A smile flitted over her face as she looked at Patsy. "I gave it to you."

"An' shot that other guy?"

"You saw me."

"After decoyin' us here where they'd get us?"

Her smile vanished. "I did not decoy you here."

"I'd like to know what you did then?" Jim demanded grimly. "You admitted it."

"Stupid, both of you!" She stamped her foot, flashed at Patsy: "Watch the stairs! They will try something!" And then she said rapidly to Jim: "I thought you would understand. I had to act that way or they would have tied me up. I wanted to be free to do what I could for all of us. So I pretended I brought you here. They did not know we were coming. They saw the lights turn off the main road, flashed a signal out of the upper window, and when we did not answer it they knew we were strangers. So they waited outside and trapped us when we slipped up to the house. But after I finished talking they thought I had brought you here to help them. They were a little suspicious, but not enough to keep me a prisoner too. You see? And the first chance I got to help you, I did."

"Well, I'll be a one-armed garbage collector!" Patsy breathed. "Ladies always did make me dizzy."

Without warning the lights in the hall below went out. Feet slithered softly. A sudden blast of shots tore up out of the darkness into the lighted hall above.

Patsy ducked, fired three times and dodged back, hunching his shoulders against the rain of plaster falling from above.

"The dirty low-lifes!" he bawled. "Springin' a trick like that!"

The crashing fusillade of shots kept up, making it impossible to approach the stairs. But all smashed into the ceiling above.

"Is this the only way down?" Jim asked Juanita.

"No! Quick! This way! I forgot! There are stairs!"

She ran lightly toward the rear of the hall. Jim and Patsy kept with her; Jim's right arm was still good. He took the gun from Patsy as they went.

A head and shoulders bobbed out from the rear stairs. Jim leaped in front of Juanita and shot an instant before the other did, emptying the automatic in one crashing roll of fire.

The man stumbled into the hall, pitched forward on his face. It was Romero. As Jim bent over him Romero rolled over with a gasping effort and tried to lift the automatic still clutched in his hand. The effort was too much. Jim snatched it away from him.

Blood was pouring out of the man's neck, welling out of his mouth. He choked something in Spanish. A smile contorted his face as he looked up at Juanita. A shudder ran through him and then his eyes slowly closed.

"Dead!" Juanita exclaimed with a catch in her voice.

"Dead," Jim agreed.

He was beginning to feel dizzy and weak from loss of blood. Pain was stabbing through the shattered shoulder. He gave it no thought now. Once more he had a loaded weapon. He started down the stairs.

"Don't go down there!" Juanita cried.

"If we don't go after them, they'll come after us!" Jim threw back, and slipped down the steps as silently as possible.

The firing in the front of the house had stopped. Dead silence greeted him as he came into a dark room, saw the glimmer of starlight through a window glass. Edging forward he bumped against a stove and knew he was in the kitchen. He heard Patsy moving behind him.

They both stopped as furtive steps sounded near. A door across the room creaked as it opened. Dim figures appeared, silhouetted against a faint light beyond. They filed into the kitchen, three of them, feet scraping softly.

A light switch clicked. A light overhead flashed on.

"Stick 'em up!" Jim shouted, crouching with gun ready.

And beside him Patsy spat: "Drop them guns!"

Patsy had an automatic in his hand also. The empty one Jim had discarded, useless now. But it looked as formidable as if it were loaded.

THREE figures faced them—the dapper dark little man who had helped hold Patsy, the taller slimmer one who had clutched Jim's left arm while Romero held the right, and Daly. All three had guns. Two of them automatics, Daly a revolver.

In the bright light that filled the kitchen the two parties faced one another. A terrible pregnant silence fell. The electric tension of death was in the air. One had the feeling that every man there was afraid to move lest he start guns roaring and lead flying.

The dapper little man gulped and lowered his weapon slowly. Fear crept over his face. His companions hesitated. Daly's thin face was drawn with animal anger. His eyes blazed hate.

"Drop those guns!" Jim ordered through tight lips. The words struck on the silence with the brittle force of steel tapping the rim of a wine glass.

Jim's eyes were on Daly as he spoke. There the danger lay. Daly would make the break if any of them did. A headlight beam stabbed through the window as an automobile approached the house. Jim saw the flame of purpose in Daly's eyes, was warned as the man's revolver jerked up and centered on him. Jim squeezed the trigger of his automatic. It leaped in his grip as it exploded.

And the revolver spun from Daly's hand and he staggered back. A crimson spurt of blood welled out from shattered fingers and spattered on the floor.

Two automatics struck the floor as their owners dropped them and raised their hands swiftly. Patsy dived forward and collected the guns. The squeal of brakes sounded at the side of the house at the same time.

Patsy straightened up, between Jim and Daly for an instant. Daly seized the chance, leaped back through the doorway and fled. Jim sprang after him, snapping: "Watch these men, Patsy!"

He came out in a hallway just as a door at the end of it slammed behind Daly. Jim reached the door in half a dozen steps, kicked it open and rushed into the front hall.

Daly was already out the front door. Jim caught a glimpse of struggling figures on the front porch. And as he made for the door Daly was shoved back in—the stocky figure of Beef Miller propelling him. Two other men crowded in after them. One Jim recognized as the man who had been with Beef Miller at the Dorringtons'. They were plainclothes men.

Miller recognized him and shouted: "Drop that gun, Reilly! What the hell are you doing here?"

Jim reversed the gun, smiling crookedly. "Glad to see you, Miller," he said, holding it out. "How in the devil did you happen along?"

"Headquarters got a telephone call from a woman to get here as quick as possible and we'd find the killer of Rodney Dorrington!" Miller snapped. "What do you know about it?"

Jim remembered then the telephone call Juanita had been making, and the last of his doubts about her were swept away.

"I didn't know anything about it until now," he confessed. "She's here, and you're holding the chap who killed Dorrington."

"You lie!" Daly snarled. "You killed the man yourself!"

Miller scowled at Jim. "Were you there?" he exploded.

"Guilty," Jim grinned. "Want to see my hands without gloves?"

For a moment it looked as if Miller was going to have apoplexy.

"So that was you!" he finally got out in a strangled voice.

Before he could say any more the hall door opened and Patsy herded his prisoners in.

Beef Miller stared at Patsy and recognized him. "Looks like old-home week!" he remarked, and then his head jerked around as two people came slowly down the stairs. It was Juanita and the elderly man Jim and Patsy had found in the attic room. Juanita was assisting him tenderly.

"Are you the woman who called headquarters?" Miller barked as they reached the bottom of the steps.

"I am," she agreed calmly. "Who are you?"

"Detective Miller from Miami headquarters," Miller growled. "Who are you?"

"I am Senorita Alvarez, and this is my father, Don Alvarado Alvarez. You may have heard of him. General Alvarez, former commander of the army of the Republic of Costuria. Now in exile from his country."

Beef Miller blinked. "Is t h a t straight?" he snapped.

The old man drew himself up and threw his shoulders back. "It is," he stated coldly. "The State Department in Washington will identify me."

Miller scratched his head, smoothed his stubby iron-gray mustache and looked puzzled.

"What's behind it all?" he demanded. "How does the Dorrington killing connect up with this racket here?"

"I think I can explain," Juanita said, flashing a reassuring glance at Jim. "Dorrington was killed by that man." She indicated Daly.

"She's lying too!" Daly spat, gripping his injured hand. "They're trying to frame me! And by God, they won't get by with it!"

"I do not lie," Juanita answered with a lift of her chin. "He was hired, Mr. Miller, by a man who lies dead upstairs, Senor Romero, whose fortune and estates were confiscated when the present government came into power, through Rodney Dorrington's money and influence. Everyone who opposed their exploitation of the country was driven

into exile—or killed. My two brothers died in prison last year."

HER voice went unsteady at that and her eyes flashed. But she spoke on rapidly.

"In this country some of the exiles gathered, trying to find a way to break the power that was bleeding their country for the benefit of the few. My father met Romero in Miami, spent much time at this house which Romero had taken for headquarters. There was much wild talk. Misfortune had affected Romero's mind, and those with him were as unsettled. Rodney Dorrington was at Miami Beach for the winter season, and my father called on him to plead for Dorrington's help in straightening out the affairs of our country. There was quite a bit of correspondence between them.

"Romero found it out, suspected my father was letting Dorrington bribe him. He made threats, and it was a long time before he could be convinced that my father had not done such a thing. This morning in Miami Romero confided to my father that they had finally decided to fix everything by removing Dorrington.

"He had met this man Daly in Miami, recognized him as a man who had been arrested in our country for murder, and had hired Daly to kill Dorrington. They had found out that Dorrington was to be dressed as a devil tonight and had obtained an admission card to the affair. Daly was to go dressed as a devil also. My father refused to have anything to do with it, and Romero flew into a rage, warned him not to interfere, and left.

"My father came to our hotel and told me about it. He did not know what to do. This afternoon he decided to go out and see Romero and try to make him change his mind. And he did not come back.

"I was afraid then they were keeping him. I did not know what to do. My father had not wanted the matter taken to the police. And I did not think they would dare hurt him. Dorrington had sent us cards to the affair, out of politeness. I finally sent a warning to Daly at the hotel Romero had told my father Daly was staying at. It must have missed him. And then I went to Dorringtons' this evening to watch for a man in a devil's suit. I saw one finally and was sure it was Daly. I warned him again and said that I would be watching him. I was certain he would not dare do anything after that.

"But Rodney Dorrington was killed after all. I saw the man I thought was Daly escaping out of the back of the house. I followed him to his car, was going to turn him over to the police. He took my gun away, forced me in his car and drove away with me. And then told me that he had not killed Daly, but had been there when it happened, so that he would be blamed for the murder. He said the murderer had taken a lot of papers, money and valuable jewelry, and among those papers were some he wanted badly.

"I believed him, and realized that in the papers taken were probably some of the letters that my father had written to Dorrington. If Romero saw them he would be certain my father had sold out to Dorrington, and might do something violent. So I brought this man and his friend here."

And Juanita quickly and calmly finished her story with an account of what had happened after their arrival, stressing Daly's return with the stolen papers.

Beef Miller listened in frowning silence, now and then tugging at his stubby mustache. At the end he barked at Jim: "How about all that?"

"True, as far as I know."

"What were you doing at Dorrington's? You didn't have any business there. Up to your old tricks again?"

Jim shrugged. "In a way, I suppose, Miller. Dorrington was a great hand to get something on a person and then use it for a club. He did that to a lady. Put her in a position where he could wreck her reputation. Had the letters in her handwriting to do it. She was engaged to a friend of mine to whom I was under deep obligation. He came to me all broken up. I weakened and said I'd get the letters for him.

"They were in Dorrington's safe. He had taken them out and shown them to the lady only a day or so ago. I decided the best way to get them was to attend the party tonight with Patsy here, slip up to the safe while everyone was busy below, open it and get the letters. And I had the bright idea of going as a devil too. It certainly tangled things up."

Jim recounted what had happened after he and Patsy arrived at the Dorringtons'.

"There I was, holding the sack for the killing," he finished. "Dorrington's wife had seen my face. You had talked to me. Not a soul in the world would believe someone else killed Dorrington and lammed. There was nothing to do but lam too. And then when Miss Alvarez showed up at the car I decided to use her to get track of the killer. It worked. Almost too well. I thought the lot of us were going to get the same thing Dorrington did."

"It sounds like a pack of fairy stories," Miller grunted. "You'll need more proof than that, Reilly. You're in bad."

"A damn lot of proof!" Daly snarled. "If you think you're going to get up in court and tell a yarn like that and kick me over with a murder rap, you don't know your law. Laugh that off!"

Jim grinned. "I don't," he said. "But you'll get the rap just the same. Patsy's got your gun there with your prints on it. The bullet that killed Dorrington can be matched to it."

"There's no gun of mine there!" Daly sneered. "I never had one. That's your gun."

"Maybe," said Jim drily. "But there's a bullet out of it in my shoulder. When you can make a jury believe I shot myself with my gun you'll have a better lawyer than you can hire. Laugh that off."

Daly glared at him, white and silent. And Jim said to Miller, "Look in his car. See if you don't find the silencer in it. And if you look close you may find the jewelry and money he walked out with. He probably expected to hold out on that. You'll find Mrs. Dorrington's necklace by the back porch steps where I tossed it."

Miller said to one of his men "Search that car out there."

The man went out, returned in a few moments with a silencer for a revolver and the stolen articles.

Beef Miller nodded his head at the sight. "You're lucky, Reilly," he growled. "You never were so close to a murder rap before. And you better never get so close again. You might not get out of it like you seem to have done this time."

"Then you will not arrest him for murder?" Juanita cried.

"Nope," Miller growled. "I've got a hunch he won't get arrested for anything this time, seeing how he's helped get the right man."

"Oh, I'm so glad!" Her dark eyes smiled at Jim.

And Jim grinned at her, and then at Miller.

"My lucky night," he said softly. "Lucky all the way around. Come on, cop, take me in town and cut the evidence out of my shoulder. I've got lots of things I want to do."

"I touched him on the shoulder. His head kind of fell forward. Then I saw the knife—"

The Corpse In Row 2

by

Maxwell Hawkins

The final close-up had faded from the screen, ushers had shut the doors, put out the lights. But there, in an aisle seat, a crumpled form remained, staring with sightless eyes at the empty silver-sheet—the hilt of a dagger protruding from his breast.

DETECTIVE Sergeant Tim Gregg, of the homicide squad, stood inconspicuously at one side of the dazzling entrance to the Corona Theatre. The special midnight showing of the sensational gangster picture, "Allies of Death," had just ended.

None of the chattering patrons who streamed from the playhouse, however, noticed the lithe figure of the detective. His neatly fitting gray suit seemed to melt into the shadows of the building—instinctive camouflage on his part.

Gregg, on the other hand, ran rapid and observing eyes over the crowd. Everyone from the slightly "jingled" fat man in evening clothes to the willowy girl with the too yellow hair received a quick scrutiny.

The detective was seeking no one person in particular. But he had been lured to the entrance of the big theatre by a hope that he might find a few persons in general—persons whom he and all the other members of the department had been anxious to lay eyes and hands on for some time now.

Gregg's knowledge of gangster psychology had more than once enabled him to make brilliant coups, to bring within the law's grip certain long-hunted public enemies. It was his reason for loitering outside the Corona Theatre at one-thirty in the morning.

The vanity and curiosity of the men he was after, so he figured, might bring some of them to see the gang film all the picture fans were raving about. And the special midnight performance was the most likely one for them to attend. It fitted into their nocturnal mode of life.

For once, however, Gregg's hunch appeared to be worthless.

The emerging stream of patrons diminished to a trickle. Then it stopped. All but a few of the lights in the entry were turned off, and he saw a gaily uniformed usher closing the row of doors that led into the house.

With a resigned shrug, the detective strolled out from his place of observation. Near the ticket booth, where a girl with red hair and a flippant manner presided when the theatre was open, he paused.

The girl was gone; the booth was dark. Gregg had seen her leave just as he had arrived to take up his vigil. She had made her way into the theatre accompanied by the elaborately uniformed doorman. They had carried a black bag—the receipts of the evening.

He stood for a second looking at the photographs depicting scenes from "Allies of Death," which were arranged in a glass case against the ticket booth. Then a slow, faintly disdainful smile touched the corners of his mouth.

"So that's the Hollywood notion of these rats," he murmured. "Well, I'd like to have some of that movie outfit with me when——"

He halted his meditations, his whole attention caught by one of the photos in the case. The smile was replaced by a grin.

"That bird's a dead ringer for 'Pig' Albini," Gregg chuckled. "Gave me quite a start for a minute."

Pig Albini was one of a half-dozen men Tim Gregg was especially anxious to bump into—or bump off, if given sufficient excuse.

The detective turned away slowly and started down the street. But suddenly he stiffened into an attitude of tense listening.

His ears, attuned to all sounds out of the ordinary, had caught a low cacophony of excited voices. The tones were muffled, but there was no mistaking their near-hysteria. Men's voices, he decided, when suddenly above the other sound he heard a woman's scream.

The cry came from behind the row of closed doors barring the way into the theatre. Three quick strides and he was close to the centre portal, when it burst violently open. A tall youth in an usher's uniform shot out and barely missed running headlong into the detective.

Gregg's fingers closed swiftly on the other's arm.

"What's the matter in there?"

He saw that the usher's face, a thin and effeminate face, was ghastly white. The youth's eyes were round and staring with fright. Before attempting to answer the detective's question, he gulped several times, and when he finally found his voice, it was trembling and stuttering.

"Let—let me go!" he gasped, trying to free himself from Gregg's firm clutch.

"Where are you going? What's the hurry?"

"For—for a cop!"

"I'm a police detective!" Gregg snapped out, tightening his hold. "What's up?"

For a minute he imagined that the frightened usher was going to collapse in his arms. But the youth shook himself together.

"Thank God!" he muttered. "You'd better hurry. I'm afraid—" He stopped.

"Well?" the detective urged, heading the usher toward the door he had just popped out of. "What are you afraid of?"

"I—I'm afraid, sir, there's been a —a murder!"

WITH a swift movement, Sergeant Gregg propelled the youth, who seemed paralyzed with terror, through the door and stepped into the theatre after him.

All the house lights, the detective noticed, were ablaze. There was no one at the back of the house, but through the glass partition which separated it from the parquet he saw a group of figures down near the orchestra pit.

He surmised that they had been the source of the excited conversation of a short time before, although now they were talking in tones too low for him to hear plainly.

Gregg, the trembling usher ahead of him, strode down the middle aisle.

At his approach, two other youths in uniform, a red-haired girl, and a short, slightly built man with a shining bald head looked up. But a fifth figure, sitting in a seat on the aisle, his head slumped forward, made no movement.

"What happened?" the detective demanded brusquely.

The bald-headed man, apparently sensing the authority of the newcomer, answered. "Why—why after the performance, we found this—" he hesitated and then pointed to the limp figure in the seat. "He's dead — killed!"

"Who are you?"

"The manager. My name's Wilcox."

Gregg turned his attention to the man in the seat. He bent over the still form, and his first glance found the handle of a dagger protruding from the left side of the breast. Although the body was still warm, there was no doubt that the fellow was dead. The detective straightened up.

"All right! Let's hear what you know about this." He spoke to the manager, briskly, efficiently. In his open palm he displayed a small leather case containing his badge.

The bald-headed man shifted his gaze from Gregg's hand to his face for an instant, but the detective noticed that he avoided looking directly at him.

"About all I know is that one of the ushers came into my office on the mezzanine floor a few minutes ago in great excitement and told me to hurry down here. That a man had been killed. Miss Ambrose, who was with me checking the receipts, came along. When we got here we found this—this body."

Gregg turned inquiringly to Miss Ambrose. He saw a pretty girl in her early twenties, whose vivid blue eyes made a startling contrast with her flaming red hair. At his glance, she nodded affirmation of the manager's words.

"Who discovered him?" the detective asked, including the three ushers in his question.

"I did, sir." It was the pale youth who had almost bumped into Gregg in the entry. "After the house had cleared, I looked around to make sure no one had fallen asleep and stayed behind. We always do that. I noticed him and thought he was a sleeper. When I came down and touched him on the shoulder, his head kind of fell forward. Then I saw that knife sticking in his side." He shuddered.

"I ran back and told Tom and Joe here," the youth continued, indicating the two other ushers, "and Joe went upstairs and got Mr. Wilcox. Then later Mr. Wilcox sent me out for a policeman—and I ran into you."

Gregg nodded and gave his attention once more to the victim of the stabber. The dead man was about twenty-five, he decided, and carefully although not expensively dressed. Thick-lensed spectacles with steel rims and bows covered the glassy eyes.

"Probably why he sat so far down in front," the detective decided, noting that the seat in which the body slumped was in the second row on the left side of the aisle.

While the others watched in horrified silence, Gregg made a swift and expert search of the dead man's clothes. A bunch of keys, a half-empty packet of cigarettes, a small roll of bills, some change, and a fountain pen were all he discovered in the pockets. There was nothing to show who the man was.

The clothing itself also failed to yield any clue to his identity. The suit bore the label of a large department store; the hat was from a chain haberdashery shop and the sweat band was unmarked with any initials.

Gregg's eyes roamed from one to another of the small group. "Any of you know this man?"

They shook their heads.

His glance halted on the red-haired girl. "Do you know him, Miss Ambrose?"

"No."

"You don't recall selling him a ticket?"

"No, sir."

"Is there anyone else in the theatre now?" Gregg asked the manager.

"Why, yes. Simmons, the doorman. When Miss Ambrose and I came downstairs, we left him in the office to watch the receipts."

"Go up and tell him to come down here!" the detective ordered, pointing to the three ushers. "Then you boys stay up there and keep an eye on that money. You may as well go with them, Miss Ambrose."

WHEN they had gone, Wilcox began to wring his hands.

"This is terrible—terrible. After it gets in the papers——"

Gregg shrugged. "When it gets in the papers, you probably won't be able to accommodate half the people who try to get into your theatre, I think," he said cynically.

While Wilcox sat down in one of the seats with a worried sigh, Gregg stood with his chin cupped between the thumb and forefinger of his right hand, contemplating the figure of the dead man.

On the fellow's right was the aisle. On his left—the side from which the gruesome knife handle protruded—stretched a row of empty seats. It was probable that the murderer had struck the fatal blow while seated beside his victim, although there was a faint chance that it had been struck from behind or from in front, the detective conceded to himself. The medical examiner would be able to determine.

Gregg tried to visualize what had happened. The man with the thick glasses coming to the theatre with a supposed friend. The sudden and deadly blow in the dark. The killer quietly getting up and leaving the house.

His thoughts were interrupted by the arrival of Simmons, the doorman. The latter looked with curiosity in which there was a trace of nervous fascination from the figure in the seat to the detective—then back to the dead man.

"Grace—Miss Ambrose told me you wanted me," he said speaking to Wilcox.

"That's right." It was the detective who answered.

He surveyed the military-looking doorman, erect and somehow impressive even though he no longer was dressed in the comic-opera uniform he wore on duty.

"You've probably heard what's happened," Gregg continued. "This man here has been stabbed to death—probably by a companion who came to the show with him. Take a good look and see if you know him or recall his

entering the lobby. You stand out in front all the time don't you?"

"Yes, sir. From three o'clock until shortly after the last show is over.'

Simmons bent over slowly and stared with tight lips at the face of the corpse. When he had finished his scrutiny a few seconds later, his own countenance was as pale as death, too. He shook his head slowly.

"No, sir, I've never seen him before."

Gregg thought a minute, then asked: "You're certain?"

"Yes, sir."

"All right. I guess that's all. I hoped you might remember him—and whoever he came here with."

"You'd better go back to the office and guard the receipts," Wilcox said, looking at Gregg for confirmation.

Gregg nodded. "And tell the others that as far as I'm concerned, I won't need them any more. But I'll probably have to question them tomorrow."

When Simmons had disappeared up the aisle, the detective spoke to the manager. "Have a big house tonight?"

"No. Rather small, as a matter of fact, considering how we've been packing them in at the regular shows. But I've tried to tell the main office that there's nothing in these owl performances in this neighborhood."

"Main office?"

"Yes," Wilcox replied. "This is one of the Federal chain houses."

"If the audience was small, I don't suppose there were many people sitting this far down," Gregg ventured.

"I didn't look," the manager said, "but I'd guess there weren't a dozen people below the fourth row. You'll notice that this is a converted vaud' house. The screen's badly arranged—too near the front," he added.

"Made it easier for the murderer," Gregg mused. He suddenly became brisk. "Well, Mr. Wilcox, we'll go up to your office and I'll notify the precinct station. After the medical examiner comes, we'll have the body moved. But while he's on his way, you and I'll just go over the theatre from cellar to roof."

The detective saw the bald-headed manager hesitate.

"Would it be all right if Simmons went with you instead?" Wilcox asked.

Tim looked at him sharply. Again the little man avoided his direct gaze. Gregg's eyelids moved closer together.

"No, it wouldn't!" he snapped.

DOCTOR DUKE finished his examination of the body in the seat and stood erect, rubbing his hands slowly together.

"Dead about two hours or less. Stab wound in the interspace between the fourth and fifth ribs, penetrating the heart. Must have died instantly."

"A homicide," Gregg suggested.

"Without a doubt. No one could stab himself in that spot—at least, not while sitting down and without attracting attention." He turned to the two uniformed policemen who were standing a short distance up the aisle. "Call the morgue wagon!"

He walked to the rail of the orchestra pit, from where Gregg and Wilcox had been watching.

"Well, sergeant, who did it?"

The detective made a wry face and Doctor Duke smiled. "That's still to be determined, huh?" the medical examiner said, starting to leave.

"Just a minute, doctor!" Gregg exclaimed.

Sitting in the second seat, he beckoned to Wilcox to take the one on his right on the aisle. The manager gave an involuntary shudder, then reluctantly complied.

"If I wanted to stab Wilcox to death," Gregg said, "could I inflict a wound such as killed the man who sat in that seat behind us with my right hand?"

Doctor Duke considered only for a moment. "Absolutely not. It took considerable force to drive that blade into the heart. You're right hand is in too cramped a position."

"In other words," the detective smiled, "the murderer was a left-handed man."

The medical man nodded appreciatively. "Ten to one, he was. The average right-handed person hasn't enough control over his left arm and hand, or enough strength to bury a knife in a man's breast from the position you're in."

"Was there any chance that the death blow was struck from in front or in back?" Gregg asked.

"Not from the way the weapon was lodged in the body."

"That's what I thought," the detective murmured. "Well, we might as well be going along," he added.

As they walked up the aisle, Gregg produced a cigarette. "Got a light?" he asked Wilcox.

The manager put his hand in his right-hand coat pocket and drew forth a lighter, which he snapped on. As Gregg leaned over the tiny flame, his eyes twinkled.

THE afternoon following the discovery of the murder in the Corona Theatre, Tim Gregg sat in the office of Deputy Inspector McGraw, facing his chief.

The crime had attracted wide-spread attention. Perhaps because of its daring—the victim stabbed apparently within sight and hearing of a large audience—or a dearth of other sensational news it had set the city rooms of the papers by their ears.

"It's just as I'm telling you, Tim," the inspector said, biting into the end of his cigar. "I've got to put some other men on the case with you. The papers are howling their heads off for action. We've got to give 'em some!"

"You're boss, Matt," Gregg replied with a resigned shrug. "But all I'm asking for is a little time."

McGraw stared out the window. "Well," he said finally, "I'd like to see you come through, my boy—you've got the best record on the squad. But you don't seem to have gotten very far with this case up to now."

"I'm working," Tim replied briefly.

"Sure," the inspector agreed. "But what have you learned? The stabbing was done by a left-handed man probably. You're just about eliminated it as a job by anyone connected with the theatre, cause you've found out that none of 'em is a south-paw. It looks like the guy must have been killed by someone who went into the show with him. But no one remembers seeing him go in—so no one remembers who was with him. That right?"

"But as soon as I identify him—"

"Yeah, that'll be a big help. But in the meantime, I've got these newspaper boys on my neck."

"I think I've settled the time the killing took place."

"How's that?"

"Have you seen the picture they're showing—a gang film called 'Allies of Death'," Gregg asked.

McGraw shook his head but the detective continued.

"Just before the finish, there's a big battle. Machine guns—hell of a racket. And even if the picture is a lot of bunk, nobody but a blind man could keep his eyes off the screen during that excitement, understand?"

Gregg saw that he had his chief's attention and continued.

"That means that the killer'd been to the show before—knew when his best chance was coming."

Guess you're right," McGraw agreed.

"I was standing in front of the Corona last night when that scene was taking place. So if the killer came out the front entrance, as he probably did, I must have had a look at him, because I was giving the crowd the once-over.

"I can remember faces. As soon as we identify this bird, and I get a look at some of his friends—" He left the sentence unfinished, but the inspector caught his meaning.

"All right, Tim," McGraw said slowly. "I'll give you until eight o'clock this evening to make a pinch. After that, some of the other boys go on the job with you. I don't want to put 'em on, but I've got to."

"Thanks, Matt," Gregg said.

He got up from his chair, but as he started for the door, the telephone on the inspector's desk rang. McGraw made a motion for him to wait, and took down the receiver.

"Hello. . . ." There was a long pause, while the inspector listened with squinting eyes. "Well, that's great! Hold the line a minute."

He turned to Gregg with a grin. "There's your break. They've found out at the morgue who your man is. His roommate just came in. Talk to them."

Gregg seized the phone with eager hands.

"This is Sergeant Gregg. Say, I want you to hold that man till I get there!" He hung up with a snap. At the door, he turned toward McGraw. "Till eight o'clock, eh, chief?"

FIFTEEN minutes later, Gregg walked up the short flight of stairs leading into the city morgue. The depressing atmosphere of that abode of death, however, failed to chill his spirits. On the contrary he moved with a quick and eager step.

"Where's the man who identified the Corona corpse?" he asked one of the attendants. "I'm Gregg, of the homicide squad."

The man waved an arm in the direction of a closed door. "In there with the assistant coroner."

There were two occupants of the private office the detective entered, one of whom he at once recognized as Potter, the assistant. The other, who was slumped in an arm chair and looked as if he might have been weeping, was a young man in his twenties. He stared at Gregg with lack-lustre eyes. Potter, however, leaped to his feet and shook his hand vigorously.

"Hello, sergeant! We've been waiting for you. This is Mr. Coleman, who identified the young fellow who was killed in the theatre last night."

COLEMAN jerked his tall gangling form out of the chair and extended a limp hand.

"Glad to meet you," Gregg said, and added to himself, "Yes, sir, I certainly am!" Then aloud: "Sit down. Have a cigarette."

The detective offered his pack. Coleman took one and as he touched a match to it, his hand shook. When Gregg had his own puffing saitsfactorily, he turned to the young man.

"You're sure about the identification?"

"Yes, sir. I—I've been rooming with him since last fall."

"The man who was killed at the Corona Theatre last night, whose body you've just looked at, was—was—"

Potter pushed a sheet of paper across the table toward Gregg. The detective consulted it for a moment, then read to Coleman: "James W. Easton, twenty-six, student at City University, home address Bellmore, Ohio. That right?"

"Yes."

"You roomed with him—where?"

"Dennison Dormitory. We were both studying for the master's degree. We met last year and became pretty good friends, so this year we decided to bunk up together."

Gregg tilted his chair back and looked steadily at the student. "Coleman," he said slowly, "were you with your roommate last night—prior to his death?"

The young man took a deep breath before answering. "Yes, sir."

"Where?"

"We ate together in a cafeteria uptown about eleven o'clock. We'd been studying all evening up till then. After we ate, I decided to go home and turn in, but Jim wanted to take a walk and get some fresh air, he said."

"Instead, he went downtown to the midnight show at the Corona," Gregg suggested.

"So it seems," Coleman agreed. "When he didn't come back last night, I was worried about him. Then I saw the description of the man who was killed in the theatre in the early editions of the afternoon papers. I hurried down here and—" He stopped with a suppressed sob.

"Tell me what sort of a fellow Easton was," Gregg asked casually. "What did he do with his spare time? Did he step out now and then? You know. Any drinking, and skirts—girls? Who were his friends out there at the university?"

Coleman thought it over. "Well, he was a pretty quiet guy," the student said at last. "Spent most of his time studying—almost wrecked his eyes sticking too close to his books. He didn't drink, I know, and I doubt if he ever had a date with a girl in his life.

Not since he came to the university, any-way.

"You see, he was trying to complete his work for a degree in less than the usual time, and that didn't leave him much leisure. About the only recreation he took was walking and an occasional movie. That's why I thought it kind of funny——"

"Funny?" Gregg's voice cut in sharply.

"Yes, sir."

"What was funny?"

"Maybe I should have said odd. The way he acted this last week or so."

"How'd he act?" There was a note of impatience.

"Why—why every evening about eight o'clock he'd make some excuse and go out. At first I suggested I'd go with him, but he made it plain he wanted to be alone. So I took the hint," Coleman replied.

"I tried to find out what it was all about after he did it the first few times —tried to kid him into telling me— but he was mum as a clam, so I let it drop. Jim wasn't the kind of a guy who'd let you pry into his affairs, if he didn't want them pried into."

"And where, Coleman, do you think he went?" Gregg asked.

"I—I——" the young man hesitated. "Well, sergeant, at first I guessed that maybe he'd fallen for a girl at last and was trying to keep it from me. He was bashful. Later I began to think that he was doing something—had a job in the evenings, maybe—that he was ashamed to tell me about."

"Like what?" the detective urged.

"Oh, I don't know exactly. Working in a speakeasy, or something like that." He shook his head. "I shouldn't talk like this about poor Jim. But—but it's just the idea that went through my head."

"What made you think he might have a job?"

"Well, once or twice he let drop a word that showed he wished he had more money. His folks only could afford to send him just enough to scrape by on."

For a short time, Gregg's expression became almost sleepy. Then he snapped out of it and stood up. He crunched out his cigarette in the ashtray and turned to Coleman.

"Come on!" he exclaimed. "The best thing you and I can do is to go out to your room and have a look at Easton's possessions. Much obliged to you, Potter."

"Ever go to the movies yourself?" the detective asked as he and Coleman descended the steps of the morgue.

"Oh, sure. Once or twice a week," the student replied.

STANDING at the curb near the campus of City University, Gregg pulled out his watch. It was seven o'clock. A faint wrinkle appeared between his eyes, then vanished.

The afternoon, which had begun so auspiciously, had proved a bitter disappointment, although the detective allowed no trace of his feelings in that regard to show.

A thorough search of Easton's things had failed to produce any tangible clew to the murderer. Coleman's description of his late roommate as a studious, unassuming individual had been borne out. The contents of the dead youth's desk had shown his only correspondence to have been with his mother and father in his Ohio home, excepting a few inconsequential and impersonal items.

Coleman had supplied Gregg with a list of the dead student's acquaintances. But the detective's questioning of such of them as he had been able to locate had proved unenlightening. Apparently, the last person to see Easton alive had been his roommate.

"Somebody," Gregg murmured softly, "is probably lying."

With a suspicion of a sigh, he turned slowly, and, deep in thought, started down the street. Suddenly he wheeled. Almost at a run, he headed for the subway kiosk two blocks away.

The red head of Miss Grace Ambrose was plainly visible in the ticket booth of the Corona Theatre as Sergeant Gregg, approached it fifteen minutes later. When she caught sight of him, he fancied that her already wide blue eyes grew perceptibly wider.

But there was nothing in his appearance to provoke any such sign of alarm. Indeed, his clean-cut features were lit up with a friendly smile.

"Eaten yet?" the detective asked.

She seemed surprised at the question. "Why—why, no I haven't."

"Come on and have a bite with me," he suggested.

"I—I only have half an hour."

"That's all right. Only have a little time to spare myself."

Again she hesitated, but there was something in the level way he was now looking at her that made the invitation appear to be a command—a command she was afraid to refuse. Her eyes dropped.

"Well—if you'll wait just a minute while I get one of the ushers to take my place."

Throughout the meal, which they ate in a secluded booth of a restaurant around the corner, Gregg carefully avoided the subject of the murder. Miss Ambrose, however, merely toyed with her food. Her companion's efforts to allay her nervousness fell on fallow soil.

Finally, as her cigarette butt sizzled in the dregs of her coffee cup, she said: "I'm sorry, but I'll have to be getting back to the theatre."

She started to rise. He detained her with a slight pressure on her arm, and when he spoke his voice was low, but it was razor-sharp.

"Miss Ambrose, why did you lie to me?"

"Lie to you? Why—why I don't understand. What do you mean?"

Her attempts at indignation failed miserably. Gregg's hand pressed more firmly on her arm.

"You lied to me when you said you didn't know Jim Easton—the man who was murdered in the Corona Theatre last night!"

For a second, tears seemed about to burst forth. Gregg's voice, however, soothing and friendly, caused her to recover her poise.

"Come, come," he said. "You've nothing to be afraid of. I know all about it, so you might as well tell the truth. It'll save you trouble in the long run."

She drew herself up, attempting to free her arm from his grip. "Are you trying to—to insult me?"

Tiny wrinkles creased the corners of the detective's eyes. He laughed briefly. When he spoke, his voice was even, but filled with meaning.

"Miss Ambrose, when you came down from the office to the main floor of the theatre with Wilcox last night, you already knew that a man had been found dead. If you didn't know Easton, why did you scream when you saw the body?"

Nervously she wadded her handkerchief with her free hand and pressed it against her cheek.

"All right! I lied to you!" the girl exclaimed suddenly. "What of it? I had a right to lie, if I wanted to, didn't I?"

He ignored her question. "Why did you lie?"

"If you must know, it was because I was afraid of losing my job."

"Losing your job?" The detective was plainly puzzled.

"Yes. Mr. Wilcox has been looking for an excuse to fire me for some time. I—I knew if my name got mixed up in this as a friend of Jim's, it would be just what he wanted."

This was an unexpected angle to Gregg. "Why should be want to fire you?" he asked.

"Because—well, because I wouldn't go out with him. Don't you understand?"

She was beginning to sob softly. "I wouldn't make dates with any of the men where I work. Tom, Joe—any of them! They all wanted to make a date. Even Simmons, and he was furious when I refused to let him."

SHE dabbed at her tear-filled eyes with her wadded handkerchief, while Gregg waited patiently.

"Of course, I understand—a lot," he said soberly. "But how about Easton?"

"He was different. I never saw him in my life until a week ago, and I didn't notice him especially at first. Then I saw he was coming back several times to see the same picture. I'm not dumb. I knew why from the way he looked at me.

"He finally got up enough courage to speak to me. Then he asked me to go out when I was through work and have some chop-suey. Well—I did. I liked his looks—his manner.

"I was going out with him to dance after the show last night," she murmured. "Now may I go back to the theatre?" she asked.

Gregg stood up. "Certainly. I'm sorry I had to upset you this way," he said kindly. "You should have told me all this sooner. I'll walk back there with you."

When he had left Miss Ambrose at her post in the ticket booth, the detective passed on into the theatre. A minute later, he rapped sharply on the door of the manager's office on the mezzanine floor. It was opened by a tall man with a waxed mustache.

"Wilcox here?" Gregg asked.

"I'm sorry, but he's not."

"When'll he be back?"

A dry smile flashed across the face of the tall man. "Oh, not for a long time—I imagine."

"Cut the stalling!" the detective snapped. "I'm Sergeant Gregg, of the homicide squad."

The other man's manner changed abruptly. "That's different!" he exclaimed. Then he lowered his voice. "Why, you should know about it. Wilcox has been arrested—"

"What!" Gregg was dumfounded.

"Yes. Two of your men took him away about an hour ago."

The detective whipped his watch from his pocket. The hands stood at a quarter to eight.

"By God! I never thought Mc Graw'd do me that way!"

Without waiting to hear more, he turned and dashed down the stairs to the main floor. In front of the theatre, he raised his arm at a passing taxicab.

As Gregg reached for the door handle, a tall figure stepped in front of him and whisked the door deftly open. He looked up and saw that it was Simmons, the doorman.

"Thanks," the detective muttered, and got in.

The cab door slammed. But before the driver could slip the car into gear, his passenger reached through and touched him on the shoulder.

"Hold it a minute!" he ordered.

Then he called through the open window of the cab to Simmons.

"Come on with me. I think I'll need you!" Gregg exclaimed.

Simmons shook his head. "I'm sorry, sir, but I can't very well——"

"You heard me! Are you going to come without a fuss, or do I have to arrest you and drag you along?"

The doorman still hesitated, but another glance at the detective's set jaw settled the matter. Simmons climbed into the cab and dropped into the seat alongside Gregg.

As the driver obeyed instructions to head for police headquarters, the detective leaned forward and closed the window that separated the front seat from the rear of the cab. Then he settled back comfortably on the cushions and began to talk to the doorman.

In contrast to his earlier talk with Miss Ambrose when he had studiously avoided the subject of the murder, he now seemed possessed with it as material for conversation. As if half to himself, he went over the whole affair from the beginning.

"It must be a horrible feeling, Simmons," the detective purred. "To be sitting there, all unsuspecting the way Easton was, then suddenly feel the agonizing thrust of a knife blade like——"

Gregg's hand had been fumbling with the upper left-hand pocket of his vest. As he spoke, his arm suddenly described a swift arc.

Simmons let out a shriek of abject terror. His mouth dropped open and his eyes seemed about to pop from their sockets.

THERE was fire in Tim Gregg's eyes as he entered Inspector McGraw's office. In his hand, he was holding his watch.

"One minute of eight," the detective said. "Well, Matt, you didn't give me much of a break——but I've delivered."

McGraw caught the hostility in the younger man's voice. "What do you mean?"

"I've got the Corona Theatre stabber. Down in a cell!!"

The inspector jumped to his feet. "By jimminy, Tim, that's great. Who is he?"

"Simmons, the doorman."

"Are you sure?"

"Sure? Well, he confessed to the whole thing coming down in the taxi."

"Let's hear about it," the inspector said, dropping back into his chair and opening a drawer of his desk. "Have a cigar?"

The detective brushed the proffered perfecto aside. "No, thanks. Here's what happened——in spite of your sending a couple of the boys out to ball things up by pinching Wilcox——"

"Why, Tim," McGraw interrupted, "about Wilcox——"

"Never mind. You and I've been friends long enough so that you'll let me tell my story. Then you tell yours," he added dryly.

"All right, Tim, my boy, go right ahead," he said quietly.

In rapid, staccato fashion, Tim gave his superior the story of his movements.

"What made you suspect Simmons?" McGraw asked.

"First, because he didn't tell the truth about knowing Easton. That is, by sight. Neither did Miss Ambrose. But her reason seemed convincing."

"That was only a suspicion, though," the inspector suggested.

"Yes, but——" The detective suddenly changed the subject. "Do you know that the rear doors of all taxicabs ——all closed automobiles, for that matter, I guess——swing backwards?"

McGraw looked at his young detective in astonishmemnt. Then a grin curled his lips. "Why, no. Do they?"

"They certainly do. For two reasons. One is so the driver can reach the handle without getting out of the cab. The other is for the convenience of the passenger. If the door opened forward, he'd have to close it, or walk around it before he could reach the driver to pay him his fare."

"By George, you're right! But what's that got to do with this case?"

"Plenty. Suppose you were a doorman, opening and closing car doors, helping passengers in and out all day long. You'd soon get on to the easiest and least awkward way to do it, wouldn't you?"

"Naturally," McGraw agreed.

"Well the easiest and most natural way *is with the left hand!*

"Simmons was naturally right-handed—but he's been a doorman for ten years and was more adroit in some respects with his left hand than with his right. The motion of opening and closing an automobile door isn't such a whole lot different from the one used in sinking a knife into a man who's sitting on your right in a theatre!

"I'll admit it didn't occur to me— until Simmons flipped open the cab door for me when I started down here. Then I brought him along."

"How'd you get the confession?"

"Primed him with talk. Then at the right moment, I pulled out my fountain pen and jabbed him with the butt, just as he jabbed Easton! He let out a yell and folded up. After that, he babbled.

"Simmons stabbed Easton to death because of that red-headed dame in the ticket booth. She went out with the young fellow, but gave him the cold shoulder. He was crazy jealous.

"He had the knife on him when Easton went into the midnight show last night—been brooding over the thing. Half an hour before the picture was over, Simmons walked into the theatre with the girl to guard the receipts.

"The employees change from their uniforms in a dressing room under the stage. After Simmons had put on his street clothes, he looked through the door into the orchestra pit and spotted Easton sitting in the second row.

"He came up, and slipped into a seat beside him, knowing there would soon be a noisy exciting scene, perfect for his purpose. Well, you know the rest, except that after Simmons had killed Easton, he went up to the manager's office as usual to stand watch."

McGraw, jubilant with admiration, walked from his seat behind the desk and placed his arm about the shoulder of his favorite detective.

"That's damn fine work, Tim!" he exclaimed. "I'm proud of you!"

Gregg was moodily silent.

"Now hear my story," the inspector continued with a chuckle. "Wilcox wasn't pinched because of the Corona murder. He was picked up on a warrant sworn out by the Federal Chain Theatre Company's auditor. It seems he's been pocketing a bunch of the gate money."

An expression of mingled amazement, chagrin and pleasure that what he had believed wasn't true spread across Gregg's face.

"Yep! That's it! And Tim, my boy, you thought—"

"Never mind what I thought!" the detective burst out. "Whatever I thought, I was wrong. No hard feelings?"

The inspector gave a hearty laugh.

"Hard feelings? With the theatre murderer in a cell? Not so long as there's a shamrock in Ireland!"

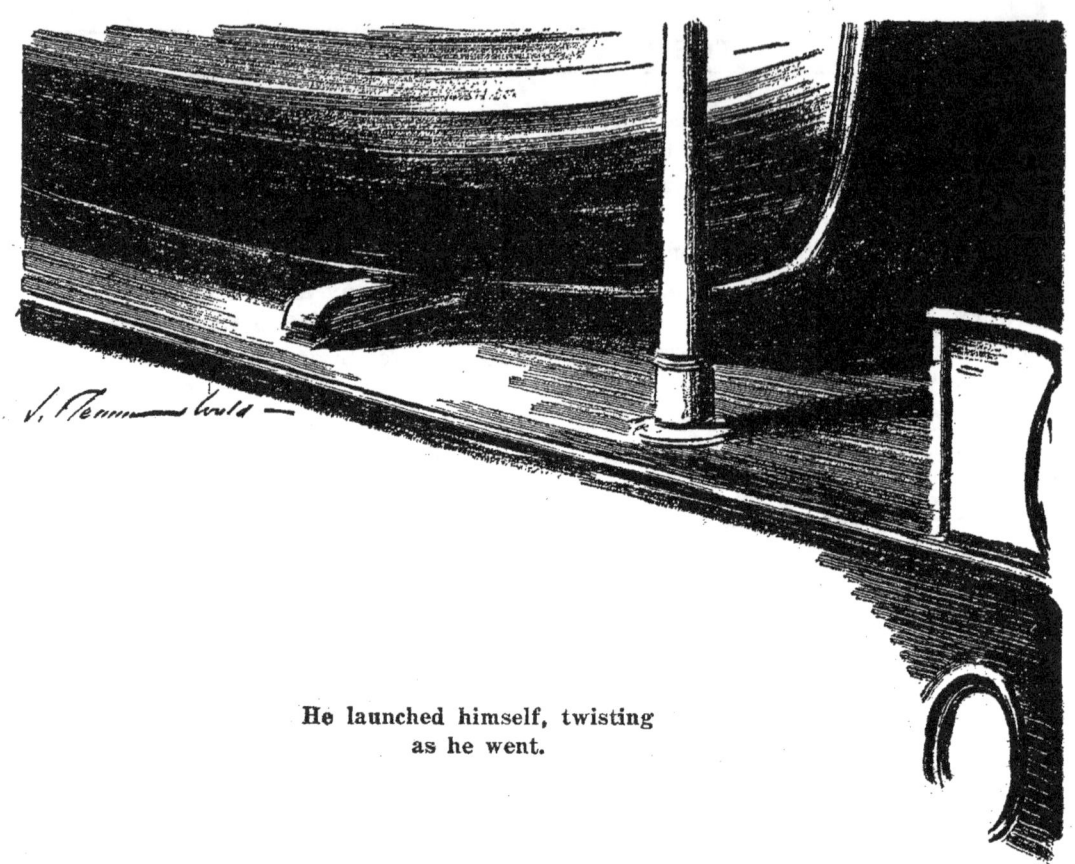

He launched himself, twisting
as he went.

The Phantom of the Porthole

by

J. Allan Dunn

Author of "The Shadow of the Vulture," etc.

Twice it had come to Mary Atchison's porthole to gibber, then fade into the night, leaving its horror-trail behind. What was this ghastly Thing with matted hair, dead flesh, an avid awful mouth? Why did it come to her—and her alone?

CHAPTER ONE

"You Are In Danger"

THE Albatross, ocean-going yacht of Russell Burthwaite, financial magnate, looked, save for her upper works and lack of armament, more like a light war cruiser than a pleasure craft as her high white hull swung at moorings in Huntingdon Harbor, Long Island. She had been built in Germany at a cost of four hundred thousand dollars and her regular crew, fore and aft, consisted of forty men.

Her tenders, and Burthwaite's commuting cruiser, in which he could make New York in a little over a half an hour, were busy conveying supplies and guests. The Albatross was going on a cruise to the Caribbean, one main object of the trip being the health of Mary Atchison, which had not been good of late. The physician who was attending her was going along. Cost was never considered by Burthwaite. It was he who said to inquiring reporters on his return from Europe: "I do not understand your question, gentlemen; I know of no depression."

He had been called the "Buffalo Bull of Wall Street" and there was a sensation when it was rumored that the bears had got him down at last, bears whose leader was Burthwaite's lifelong rival John Carling Quincy. But Burthwaite had weathered that fight, if indeed he had ever been in it. Other reports had it that he had gained another enormous fortune for being short during the panic of 1930.

A man who could be affable, who liked to be extravagantly hospitable, whether at his mansion at Huntingdon Haven or his Casa Grande at Palm Beach, his shooting chalet in Maine, his residence on Upper Fifth Avenue, or aboard the Albatross. In repose his features were not genial. His eyes could be as ruthless as his voice. It was said he asked no odds and gave no favors.

Now he was taking his niece and ward, Mary Atchison, on a cruise to restore her nerves and bring her heartbeats back to normal, if possible, by the tonic of tropic scenes and air. There were those who said Burthwaite had no heart but there was no denying the affection and attention he showed the girl, who was an heiress in her own right. Burthwaite was her legal guardian until she came of age, an event now only a month or so away. Worried by the recent condition of her health he had planned this excursion, urging her to ask her own friends, deeply solicitous of her comfort.

There was one friend Mary Atchison would have liked to have aboard, one whose presence might have proved the biggest possible tonic. But she did not mention his name. It would have been a greater irritation to the Buffalo Bull of Wall Street than any scarlet *capa* of a matador to a *toro* of the Madrid bullring—John Carlin Quincy, Junior.

Burthwaite did not even know that she had met him. If he had had any idea of how far their acquaintance had progressed until friendship had graded into love, he would have figuratively frothed at the mouth and pawed the ground. To mention the name of Quincy was to find the weak joint in the otherwise impregnable armor of Burthwaite.

Mary Atchison knew of his prejudice. She regarded it merely as a question of financial supremacy—as it was. That rating did not enter into her scheme of things. Nor into that of John Carlin Quincy, Junior. To both of them money was something that had always appeared in their lives as inevitably and naturally as the water that flowed from the taps in their bathrooms. That Quincy, Senior regarded or professed to regard, Burthwaite as a pirate, rather than a financier, was nothing to Quincy, Junior. All he knew was that he loved Mary Atchison and she loved him, both of them swept off their feet by a tide greater than any man-made current of trade and exchange.

Both respected their respective parents —Burthwaite being in loco parentis to Mary, since her own father and mother were dead. They had met accidentally perhaps, yet inevitably, at a country-club function. That had begun and fixed their own affair.

Young Quincy was worried at the state of Mary Atchison's health—and so was she. She could not understand why, vigorous, athletic, untiring, she should suddenly become languid,, inclined to fits of drowsiness alternated by long white nights of sleeplessness; know lack of energy and moments when she twitched and tossed in uninvigorating sleep.

She did not tell young Quincy of these happenings but he saw her languor, wondered at her tiring in the midst of a game, even a dance. He thought the trip might be a marvellous thing, at first, even if he was eliminated from it. Afterward, he was not so sure, following, curiously enough, a talk with his father.

DOCTOR KREIG, her personal physician, called in by Burthwaite, talked of heart murmurs, of life histories going back to earlier generations. He took analyses and, after them, said little but wrote certain prescriptions and recommended change of scene and air.

A clever doctor, Kreig, without question—but evasive. Mary Atchison challenged him to tell her what was wrong. But he put her off.

"One must not diagnose too hastily," he said. "Yours is an interesting case, one that is unique. I am privileged to study it. You must place yourself in my hands."

He left the girl with a vague idea that previous generations had left their stigma of folly and disease upon her. Above all, he told her, she must fight against melancholia and despondency.

"Fight—always," he said. "If you are strong enough—you will win. Your will—against the weakness of your body."

She had the will to live—and the will to love—but of late the depression of lax pulses followed by too swift heartbeats, swamped her. She feared the inherited traits that Kreig, under her questions, had hinted at, then depreciated.

"To your own self be true," he told her, but it did not comfort her. What if her own self had no true foundations?

She appreciated the cruise, her guardian's thought for her, and she invited a dozen of her own set who accepted eagerly.

A cruise on the Albatross represented an answer to what they craved—publicity, pictures in the society sheets, flickers in the news reels, a good time. There would be wonderful things to eat and drink, a special orchestra to dance to; Caribbean, with moonlight nights, the height and depth of luxury.

Burthwaite had invited, on his own account, certain men—their wives included, more or less necessarily—with whom and through whom he made his coups on Wall Street.

Altogether there were thirty guests aboard, luxuriously quartered. Their maids and valets were taken care of. The Albatross had been designed for just such jaunts. Its service quarters began to bustle with expert activity long before the captain gave his order to hoist the hooks that held the cruiser to the mud.

Now the tide served. The tenders were hoisted, the other craft sheered off, the powerful Deisels applied their thrusts and the twin screws churned deep, changing the water to liquid serpentine and marble, white-veined and alive with pulsations. The ship moved off majestically between the red and black buoys of the channel, making for the Sound and then the open sea. Charts showed the hidden bottoms, the power of vaporized oil laughed at wind and current. Inexorably accurate, the bow of the Albatross scored her course. Man-willed, man-made, she defied the whimsies of the elements.

A mahogany-hulled cruiser, the latest thing in elegance and efficiency, shot out from Northport, yacht burgee and private signal flying from the spreaders of its stump mast. The Albatross could make torpedo boat speed outside—almost—but in less aggressive waters the Go-Getter, registered in the name of John Carlin Quincy, Junior, could run rings about her.

Young Quincy did not do that. He was barred from the guest list of the Albatross though there were a thousand hosts and hostesses who would have made many sacrifices to entertain him. He did not make any demonstration but he dipped his private signal as he rounded the port quarters of the yacht that was carrying away all that gave to young Quincy the stimulus of happiness. Mary had told him where her own suite was situated and he caught a glimpse of her face, a scrap of waving linen at the open porthole that was a mute farewell, not a true lovers' parting but the best to be done under the circumstances. Burthwaite and Quincy were as far apart as Montague and Capulet but Quincy, Junior, could not play Romeo to Mary's Juliet these days.

Shakespeare himself could have done little with the Albatross for setting.

There was no sense in trailing the Albatross to sea, or acting as her escort. Mary Atchison was hostess to her own guests. Her face vanished from the opening and Quincy spoked his wheel on the Go-Getter as the bigger ship forged out through the main channel. There was a frown on his forehead, his eyes were troubled. He was shrewd, he had imagination, and he did not like this trip. He was not certain whether Mary Atchison might benefit from it. He had done what he could to offset his fears but it was hard to be left out of it, to be isolated from the girl he loved by the inviolable seclusion of that swiftly moving private craft.

ON the heights of the Northport shore, two men stood in a vacant space of the developing suburbs of the little seaport that had jumped in twenty years from a quiet fishing village to a place of yacht and country clubs, of lawns, garages, villas and gardens.

Presumably they were looking over the acreage with the idea of purchase and the erection of a Spanish or Italian or Colonial mansion, with terraces and formal flowerbeds, tennis courts and rose gardens. It was an ideal location for that sort of thing though the two men did not seem the kind to be likely to appreciate it.

Their faces were hard, their eyes were small, cold and pale—one gray pair with flecks of hazel, the other faint blue. One had the nose of a hawk, the other a nasal organ that had been abused like his ears. He looked like a plug-ugly, a palooka pugilist whose brains had not been improved by the batterings of his body—powerful, feral, surly brute.

The other looked equally predatory, but was far more intelligent and alert. The one might be a bulldog, this one was a hawk, far-seeing, fast-moving, ready to swoop and rend——scout rather than sentinel.

He handed over to the other the expensive binoculars through which he had been surveying the departure of the Albatross. From where they stood they could see across the Sound to the shores of Connecticut with the naked eye, and the powerful prismatic lenses of the binoculars had brought out every detail on the yacht with sharp precision.

"There they go, "Slugger'," he said. "A bunch of millionaires and a lot of dudes. Lots of pretties aboard, plenty of jack there."

"Yeah?"

Slugger's little eyes grew avid. Muscles showed suddenly along the line of his jaws as if he were chewing on a savory quid.

"Plenty of ice?" he suggested. "Those dames doll up same as on shore, don't they? Got all their junk along?"

The hawk-faced man shrugged his shoulders. "Might be good pickings there," he said. "It ain't our racket, Slugger."

"It would be one hell of a good side-line," persisted the ex-fighter. "Where do we go from here, Mason?"

"We know they're off. I understand the delay was because of some deals Burthwaite was fixing up. He's a slick operator, that bird. But now they're gone we run down to New Orleans and get in touch with Traveau. But we keep lined up with the boat through radio, see. That's all arranged for, in code."

"Traveau? The flyer?"

Mason mocked his slower witted mate. "Yep. The flyer. Not Traveau the ditch-digger, or Traveau the land-scape-gardener. Traveau the flyer."

Slugger scowled and growled. He knew he was dumb but he resented being kidded. Also not being let into the inside plans of what was going on.

"Aw! How did I know? This Traveau guy is a stunt man, ain't he? Got records. How'd I know he was in with the gang?"

"Because he's a stunt man, Slugger. And this is the biggest racket he's had a chance at, so far. Ditto with you and me. If we work this right we don't have to worry any."

Slugger's pale eyes lit up again. Once more he seemed chewing upon an invisible and palatable quid. He could see himself a heavy spender, a popular play-boy along Broadway. Slugger liked the physical things of this life.

"Just what is the racket?" he asked. "Wise me up, won't you?"

"You'll get wise O.K.," snapped Mason. "I'm handling it for the chief. Less you know, the less you'll tip off to some blonde come-on, or a brunette! They're mostly brunettes, down in New Orleans. That's some town, Slugger. They step out there, high, wide and handsome."

Slugger licked his thick lips, pulped many a time in the days when he had to take it and like it. "So they tell me," he said.

The two turned back to where they had left their car.

ABOARD the Albatross Mary Atchison was not entertaining her guests. She had gone from the porthole where she had waved to her lover, back to the bedroom of her special suite.

There had been a note pinned to her pillow, one of a dozen soft cushions of all sizes piled at the head of the bed above the orchid-hued silken coverlet. She unfastened it with the nervous shaking fingers, the swift gathering of a light dew of perspiration that, nowadays, was apt to come upon her suddenly whenever anything happened out of routine. An uncontrollable and annoying nervousness she could not shake off and found hard to fight.

The message was in ink, inscribed in neatly printed block lettering that held no individuality, all in capitals.

MISS ATCHISON;
BE ON YOUR GUARD. YOU ARE IN DANGER. IT CANNOT BE AVOIDED WHILE YOU ARE ON THIS TRIP. BE VERY CAREFUL. DESTROY THIS.
NEMO.

Nemo! Nobody! The letters had been made with precision. So far as one might judge such script as this argued someone of education as the writer. So did the using of the semicolon after her name. But she was too terrified to notice this. Normally she was far from a coward. It was not so much automatic terror as that she was in fear of fear. Now, in this note, in her condition of nerves that short-circuited, a system that failed to coordinate properly, glands that were feeble, devitalised, irregular, fear raised its horrid head like some poisonous cobra, ready to strike.

If this was a friendly warning it held no encouragement, no promise of help, it fixated the dread that sometimes gripped her when she woke in the night from brief, restless sleep.

Her will, enfeebled, or ensconced in some refuge of her brain, rallied and she wiped the sweat from her forehead and, with fingers that still trembled, measured into a glass the prescribed number of drops from a phial Doctor Krieg had given her for emergencies, she added water from a carafe, a silver thermos bottle already filled with chilled liquid. It was a bitter dose and for a moment her heart pounded like an engine that is being raced. Then she felt stronger.

She tore up the note and then regretted it. She would not destroy it. She would show it to her uncle. He was used to such matters. He had been threatened himself and, while he might affect to pooh-pooh it personally, she knew he had taken certain precautions. Surely, on this stanch ship, where there were none but friends of herself or Burthwaite, none but trustworthy employes, she should be safe.

She tested the door that led to the little private corridor of her suite. It was locked but not bolted. She had the key, her maid did not have a duplicate —only one to the outer door of the superbly fitted apartment, in which she also had a small cabin for her own use, so that she might be within call of her mistress during the night.

Mary Atchison heard Francine now, moving in the dressing room, putting away the elaborate wardrobe brought aboard. She was a Breton girl who was devoted to Mary Atchison and had been in her service for eight years. She could be absolutely trusted.

But Francine was sure that no one had been in the suite since she entered it an hour ago, before her mistress had come aboard. She was certain there had been no note on the pillows and in her excitable fashion she was indignant that anyone should have dared to do such a thing.

"Did it upset you?" she asked, speaking French anxiously.

There was color in Mary's cheeks now, sparkle in her eyes. Krieg's medicines were always wonderful stimulants though not always lasting. He deprecated using them, warning Mary not to depend upon them.

"I am all right, Francine. Say nothing about this. I am going on deck. Keep the door locked when you go out."

"I'm not likely to, m'selle. And no one shall enter."

CHAPTER TWO

Doom of the Drowned

MARY had greeted her own guests but had not yet met all of Burthwaite's. Now she received them graciously, her manner gay and spontaneous. Burthwaite smiled at her, took occasion to whisper to her.

"You are looking better already, Mary. And, as usual, a perfect hostess."

There was no opportunity, as yet, to tell him of the note. She began to wonder whether she should do so at all. She knew the financier's guests were important men, that undoubtedly the cruise, so far as they were concerned, was not entirely one of pleasure. Burthwaite might ignore the depression but here were men who could affect it and doubtless would, if only selfishly. Men of affairs, of large controls, giants of the money world.

She had read speculative articles in the press that tried to pin some definite motive on this assembly aboard the Albatross. It was only guesswork. All these, from Burthwaite down, were adepts at granting interviews and saying nothing. Burthwaite had been the one to bring them together and the Sphinx was a more likely prospect for a reporter than he was. Doubtless he had in mind some combination that might affect Europe as well as the United States, might settle the question of the next presidency. The most astute of the interviewers had hinted that these men might swing the next election regardless of party, working for principles they would promulgate as the wisest. This writer had suggested that the cruise had to do with deficits, with overproduction and dividends. It was cleverly done, that article. But the press had had to be content largely with the results of

their batteries of cameras and microphones, with descriptions of the palatial craft and the social and financial standing of the passengers.

It was a "Mystery Cruise" in the headlines.

Deft stewards saw everybody installed—refreshments passed. The machinery of the big boat moved like clockwork. An orchestra played. The guests settled down to talk or bridge—a few danced. The chef oversaw the preparation of the elaborate menu. There were flowers in every stateroom, soft-footed servants attending to every need—some private ones, others supplied by Burthwaite.

There was a smart breeze and the blue, sparkling waters of the Sound had crisp motion. Yachts bowed to the wind, or stood up to it, off the Connecticut and Long Island shores. There were lesser cruisers. A liner was headed eastward. A smaller one swung north as the Albatross, stately and serene, making nothing of the swell, turned her bows to the south, off the New Jersey coast.

It was almost two hours before Mary could get away by herself from her duties. The stimulus of the medicine had passed and fatigue pressed hard upon her with the vague depression that nowadays accompanied it—the feeling that something was about to happen. She tried to convince herself, as Krieg had done, that it was nothing but nerves out of tune but it was hard not to consider it as a genuine presentiment. She was not superstitious but she believed it might be some true phenomenon, some sixth sense that warned her. It had intensified since she came aboard, at least since she read the note whose fragments were still in her handkerchief, tucked inside the sleeve of the light sweater she was wearing.

Doctor Krieg met her, blond, spectacled, deferential but insistent. He took her hand and felt her pulse. "You have been upset," he said in his smooth voice. "You must not let anything disturb you. That is why you are aboard, and I am aboard," he said with a flashing smile of perfect teeth. "What is it?"

His discernment was almost uncanny at times, Mary thought. Perhaps it was only his skill. Burthwaite had told her he was a specialist and to have full confidence in him. But she evaded the direct question.

"Everything is going nicely," she said. "I am naturally tired. I am going to lie down."

He nodded gravely then slightly shook his head at her as if he sensed her reservation. "Do so," he said. "But be careful with those stimulants I gave you. They have reactions."

She thanked him and passed on. A wave of weakness swamped her as she reached the deck door to her suite. She leaned for a moment against the house, her eyes closed against the mist that suddenly affected them. She felt an arm beneath her elbow.

"I beg your pardon, miss. "Can I do anything for you?"

They wore smart uniforms aboard the Albatross, from captain to dishwasher. This man was a steward, in immaculate white, his title on his cap. She did not know him but men changed aboard the Albatross frequently enough. The pay was good but the yacht was often out of active commission for weeks and even months, with only a harbor crew. She liked his looks and his manner. His eyes were respectful but alert as his manner.

"I am in charge of suites A to D," he told her. "At your service, Miss Atchison, always."

He saluted and left as she entered her suite. She wondered vaguely why so smart and plainly intelligent and effi-

cient a man should be only a steward, but the tips were large, she supposed, and it did not matter. There were often times when things did not seem to matter, when her will could only be summoned by an effort, when she was overwhelmed by a feeling that nothing mattered—not even John Quincy. But she wished he could have been aboard. He was the man to look after her, to take care of her. He wanted to devote his life to it. Her uncle had his own affairs. She did not want to bother him, or to interfere with him.

SHE was met by Francine and the look in the maid's face dismissed her own trouble for the moment. She could still brace herself though it always cost her something.

Francine's honest, flat features were drawn. There were hollows under her eyes and the eyes themselves were staring, with dwindled pupils. Francine used rouge and it looked ghastly, smeared on a skin that had become the hue of putty.

"Francine, what is the matter with you? You look as if you had seen a ghost."

Francine crossed herself. "A ghost! m'selle, why did you say that? — *revenant!* Sainte Marie!"

Francine's wits were wool gathering. She had been shocked out of regard for anything but her own sensations. Mary cross-examined her.

"They say there is a ghost aboard, m'selle, one who has returned from the dead. One who seeks to reenter life by taking possession of another's body, another's soul."

Mary laughed. "What nonsense, Francine. Aboard the Albatross? Who put such silly notions into your mind?"

"That's what the doctor said, m'selle. But those things do happen. Especially when men are drowned. We, of Brittany, know it."

Mary knew the legnds of the Breton fishermen, that the drowned men returned and sought to relive by driving out the soul of some other person. *Revenants*—those who return.

"You mean Doctor Krieg?" she asked.

"Yes, m'selle. We were all called to the chief steward's room for instruction —the same as other trips. He gave us printed orders, as usual. He was starting to make a talk, like he always does, when Doctor Krieg came in. He was angry about something."

"What's all this foolishness about a drowned man haunting the ship?" he asked. "Who is it supposed to be?" The chief steward spoke up. It seems a man named Thompson was on anchor watch, m'selle, two or three weeks ago. He was missing. He used to drink on the sly and he was going to be dismissed. They think he fell overboard. And he's been seen, with his eyes shining but strange, not like eyes at all, with the color washed out of them. All seafire —*feu de mer*—the men say, who've seen him glaring through the portholes, looking for a chance to enter somebody's body while they are asleep and their souls are feeble. His hair like seaweed, m'selle."

"That is idiotic, Francine. He knew he would lose his position and he probably went ashore, for more drink perhaps, and was afraid to come back."

"He had a month's wages, almost, coming to him," answered the practical Francine, to whom money was next to her God. "He would not do that. The doctor said it was impossible, that when a man was dead he could not appear in such a shape, much less do harm—or mean it. He said that a dead man's soul goes to judgment, that it is not allowed to roam. But"—she crossed herself once more—"he is an infidel. Souls in purgatory may be *revenants*. The sailors, even those who are not Catholics know that. They have seen. Not only this one, but others."

"You are absurd, Francine," said Mary. "The doctor was right. Be a good girl and say your prayers and nothing can harm you."

Yet, in spite of her words, she felt a cold chill creep down her spine. She felt her smooth, satiny skin pimple to gooseflesh and, when Francine glanced over her shoulder at the porthole that held only the blue and golden flash of wave and sky, Mary Atchison half expected to see some dripping, bloated, phantom countenance appear.

She forced a laugh. "What else did the doctor say?"

"He forbade us to talk about it, to think of it. He said it was an order. That it was ridiculous and impossible. But you can't stop people thinking, or feeling, or talking, m'selle, about such things. I tried to. The other maids began whispering and I left them, after the instruction meeting was over. You're right, m'selle, I'll say my prayers and tell my beads in a dozen extra Aves. The Blessed Virgin wil protect. I—"

She broke off, suddenly repentant. "That I should talk of such things. With you ill."

Mary Atchison laughed again. "I don't believe in them, Francine. Nurses' tales. They do not frighten me."

She was not quite sure of herself as she went into her bedroom again to change for dinner. All values were uncertain these days. But ghosts—there were no ghosts. There might be some drunken madman aboard, revengeful, on account of dismissal. But where could he hide? It was ridiculous.

There was something else on her pillows. Not white, like the note, but dark, blue-black as an asp. It fascinated her.

Again she was gripped with fear. It was a stubby automatic pistol.

There was no message with it. She forced herself to pick it up. She was not unfamiliar with weapons. Burthwaite had one, larger than this. She had seen it one day in the drawer of his desk. His guards carried them. She was a modern girl and she could bring down a pheasant or a partridge with accuracy. This was something concrete. It was ominous but not a menace. It looked almost as if placed there for protection, an accessory to the note of warning.

She picked it up. It had a full clip and a cartridge in the breech. With swift decision she put it away in the drawer of her dressing table, among toilet aids. She did not want Francine to see it. But she meant to sleep with it under her pillow. This could have nothing to do with *revenants* but it might coincide with the note. There was something wrong aboard the Albatross.

Her heart was too fast again—fluttering. She looked at the tonic and then she took the phial and poured its contents resolutely into the basin in her de luxe bathroom.

"Krieg is all right," she told herself, "but I'm going to fight this out by myself. It's not a practical joke and I can't see what it means. But I'll take no more drugs unless I'm gasping.

"I'm taking my bath and dressing for dinner, Francine," she called cheerfully.

"Yes, m'selle," said Francine and prepared the perfumed water, laid out dainty undergarments, besought her mistress's selection of the gown for the evening. "You are in good spirits, m'selle," she said.

"One must be, Francine, when others are so foolish, like you," Mary answered.

Francine had turned on the lights but she looked with apprehension at the dark circle of the porthole. The sun had gone down. Day was over. The Albatross clove through the waves, brilliantly illuminated, powerful, seemingly invincible against any outside, malign influences.

AN hour after midnight Mary slept, one arm beneath her blond head—slept well.

At the same time two men sat in a cabin filmed with cigar smoke. Now there were few lights showing except the working ones. The sea air had sent the guests early to bed. There had been no talk of the grisly creature seeking to set its soul anew in human form among them. Dr. Krieg had spoken for Burthwaite and the employes knew better than risk their jobs by talking openly. No doubt many of them slept fearfully and fitfully but they, superficially, at least, obeyed orders.

The talk between the two men was incisive, far from friendly. They smoked and they drank but there was nothing of comradeship evident.

"What you ask of me," said the younger, "is nothing short of murder."

"There have been plenty of times when you have stopped little short of that," said the other. His even tones could hardly be called a retort. They were rather a riposte. The parry of a skilled fencer when his grating steel raspingly and deliberately offsets the thrust of an inferior, sure of supremacy, bereft of unnecessary effort.

"This is not murder," he went on. "I look for elimination—self-impelled elimination—suicide. I look to you, I pay you, to bring this about. So far it has gone well. If it comes to a satisfactory conclusion you are provided for for life, with judicious investments. A quarter of a million dollars, in cash. You have had several thousand already.

Or, of course you may quit—and wind up in the penitentiary for life. For life," he repeated viciously while the other flinched. "You have nothing to state against me that I cannot deny successfully. You have no proof. I have your record—for four years. They will penalise you for those four years with five times the count in Ossining. I will see there is no leniency in your case. Twenty years, my friend, against twenty-five times ten thousand dollars. Money—that is why you have broken the law, hitherto. Money for your lusts—"

"What about you? You, with your—"

"Never mind about me. Right now I am in the position to dictate and I so intend. Are you going through with this—or not?"

For a second or two they fought across the table, not with actual blades of steel, but with the fighting glances of their eyes. Wills, not muscles, dictated that strife of which the rules were not entirely fair.

"You devil!" said the younger man tensely. "You win."

"When you are my age, you will, if you restrain your appetites," said the elder. "You are clever but a trifle gross. As for your conscience," he sneered, "there is no hereafter, my friend. If I thought there was—"

His gaze grew fixed. He shook his head, his features twitched. "That is all," he said. "We understand each other. Good night."

The other left, went out on deck, angry but knowing himself helpless. He was a slave—pledged to a major crime. It was nothing less. If it could be proven on him he might escape the chair but not the penitentiary, and that already threatened him. He was in the power of the devil who had deliberately found out what he had done wrong and held the knowledge over his head like a sword of Damocles. He should have killed the devil just now.

His face twisted in rage, its usual placidity turned to viciousness. He snarled like an animal caught in a trap and the snarl still showed as he flicked his lighter and fired the end of a cigarette.

A figure in white came silently round the end of the house. The man passed by, saluting. It was the steward in charge of suites A to D. The other checked him.

"A fine night, steward."

"Yes, sir."

"You're up late, aren't you?" There was suspicion in his voice. This man might have been prowling, listening. Nobody could suspect anything but if they stumbled on to something—

"The shifts haven't been quite settled sir," said the steward. "I'm taking watch until eight bells. Is there anything I can do for you, sir?"

"No. I'm not feeling sleepy, that's all."

"Yes, sir. Good night, sir."

The steward disappeared; the other went to the rail.

CHAPTER THREE

The Phantom at the Porthole

THREE bells, then four were struck forward, repeated aft. All was well as the Albatross sped south. There were figures on the bridge, a lookout forward. Otherwise the decks were deserted. The moon flung the port side in deep shadow from the deck buildings. There were no lights showing at the ports. But a vague, dark form, like a condensation of the shadow, seemed to flit along and pause, almost invisible, outside the sleeping chamber of Mary Atchison.

She awoke suddenly. This time her heart seemed to stand still in the grip of fear. There was something tapping at her porthole. It was closed. Ventilation was otherwise arranged for.

The raps came again. She tried to call out but her tongue was paralyzed, her vocal cords would not function in her parched throat.

There was a faint, weird light outside the circle of thick, clear glass. It took on dim, ghastly shape—a fearful face, livid, that seemed revealed by the glow from its awful eyes. They were like twin globes of putrescence, phosphorescent, weird and horrible.

The girl groped beneath her pillow, half automatically. This thing could not come in through that glass. It could not be real. This must be nightmare. The touch of the weapon helped. She slipped out of bed and stood against the wall reaching for the switch. Beside her the grisly horror peered in with its frightful orbs. The light flashed on in the ceiling dome, not brilliant but enough to reveal other terrific details of the face of the Thing. The face of a *revenant,* risen or summoned from the deep. Matted hair, dead flesh, an avid, awful mouth.

It gibbered at her and her courage melted from lack of physical health. She managed one harsh, gasping shriek and then swooned ,the gun falling from her hand.

Francine came, frightened but swift to the rescue. The porthole was blank but Francine knew well enough what had been there—a phantom. She pressed the bell for the night steward. He appeared instantly.

"Get Doctor Krieg," said Francine. "He's in the next cabin—E."

E was not as elaborate a suite as those from A to D but it was excellently equipped and convenient to the doctor's patient. Burthwaite's quarters were in Suite A, extending across the whole width of the deck house, astern.

"Better get her on the bed first," said the steward and helped Francine lift her there. He picked up the gun and was standing with it in his hand when Krieg appeared in dressing gown and slippers.

"I thought I heard someone cry out," he said. "What is the matter? Where did you get that gun?"

"It was on the floor, sir, by the porthole."

Krieg frowned, shook his head as he bent over his patient, feeling her pulse. "You can go, steward," he said sharply. "Francine, get me the little brown bottle of tablets, quickly."

She hurried to obey, came back with the bottle. "It's empty, doctor," she said.

He took the phial and examined it with incredulity. He dropped it and lifted the closed lids, listening for heart beats. The girl was alive, was merely in a swoon, her vitality low. She had not, as he had thought, taken an overdose, after all. The pistol puzzled him.

"I'll be back in a minute," he told Francine. "Chafe her wrists."

He hurried out, returning almost instantly with a hypodermic injection which he gave her. The eyelids fluttered, taking a deep breath. Francine stood by watching.

"What's this? What's this?"

Krieg turned to see Burthwaite, grayhaired, gray-eyed, ruddy and dominant, his sturdy form swathed and girdled in a brocaded robe. The steward was behind him, remaining in the dressing room but observant.

Krieg explained briefly. "She's coming out of it," he added .

The girl confirmed it. Her eyes opened, recognized her uncle.

"What happened?" he asked anxiously.

"I'm not sure, uncle. It was silly

f me. Perhaps I dreamed it after all but it seemed as if there was a terrible face looking through the porthole."

"*Mon Dieu! Le revenant!*" cried Francine.

Burthwaite glowered. "What nonsense is this," he demanded of the shrinking maid.

Krieg enlightened him. "I happened to hear two sailors talking about it at the landing," he ended. "It did not seem much but gossip but, in the state of Miss Atchison's nerves I thought it best to speak to the captain. He suggested I should attend the stewards' instruction meeting, which I did. He said he would stop any such ideas among the men, and speak to the chief engineer."

"It must have been your nerves, my dear," said Burthwaite. "Or someone has dared to play a prank. I'll put a stop to that. It was probably just an hallucination."

She managed a smile. "I expect so, uncle. I'm sorry to have disturbed you. I'll be all right. Don't worry. Doctor Krieg will look after me."

Krieg nodded. "I'll stay with her a little while," he said. "I think you had better leave, Mr. Burthwaite."

Burthwaite went out, the steward following.

"You're a new man," said the owner.

"Yes, sir. Underwood's wife was about to have an operation. Mr. Johnson got me in his place through Filer's Agency. The name is Sheldon, sir."

"Very good, Sheldon. You were right to call me."

"I thought you'd want to know, sir. She seemed quite ill to me."

"Yes. I'll run down this ridiculous thing. No guests would do it. If it was one of the crew, I'll—" He checked himself. "It was probably a nightmare. My niece hasn't been well of

late. Looked in through her porthole, eh? Nonsense."

"Someone was standing here, sir," said Sheldon. "In naked feet. And they were wet."

THE ray of his torchlight showed the imprints of sole and heel of two bare feet, revealed by their wetness. There were other traces of water on the desk planks, as if someone, something, had stood there and dripped.

"You'll say nothing of this, Sheldon," said Burthwaite sternly. "We'll get this joker. We'll make an example of him. Tell the staff captain I want him. He'll be on the bridge. Send a quartermaster. You'll find one forward of the funnel. No crew allowed abaft. Only cabin attendants and, of course, any officer. This is reserved for passengers. My God, I'll have the cur keelhauled."

Sheldon saluted and went forward. Those wet prints had startled him, given him cause for thought.

The staff captain, actually the mate, listened to Burthwaite stolidly. He was a solid man. He was a sailor but a modern one. He did not believe in hallucinations. Navigation was an exact science, the stars and sun were regular in their courses. All was ordered law. Seafire and corposants were only luminous sea insects and electrical phenomena. Sailors' souls did not inhabit albatrosses and Mother Carey's chickens. Things moved exactly as the beating engines of the Albatross, the deviation of the compass, the reckoning, the Sumner's lines and logarithms of the day's position.

"The old man's had a spot too much, maybe," he told himself under the bronzed mask of his countenance. "But he don't offer me one, darn his hide."

"Can't believe any of the crew had a hand in it, sir," he said. "Maybe the young lady dreamed it. But I'll over-haul all hands, off and on watch, deck and engine room. That swab Thompson fell overboard, soused. I'd like to find the man who started any old woman's yarn of him, or his ghost, looking through portholes."

He went on his way to stir up the ship's company. If anybody was monkeying around they would be sorry for it.

Doctor Krieg entered as he left. "She had a gun," he said. "She said she found it. I asked her what she meant to do with it and she said defend herself."

"That's enough for tonight, Krieg," said Burthwaite abruptly. "I leave her in your hands. You understand the case. Come in," he called sharply, in answer to a knock on his door. "What is it now, Sheldon?"

"I was looking again for those wet marks on the deck, sir," he said. "There are some splashes on the side of the house, also. Most of them are water. They'll dry out and disappear. But some won't. They're blood."

"Blood?" Burthwaite stared at Krieg and Krieg at him. "Blood? You're sure?"

"Pretty sure, sir. They don't look like paint, and they're the right color. Maybe if the doctor would take a look at them——"

"Good idea. Krieg — wait — I'll come with you."

The beam of the torch showed the scarlet smears. They were unmistakeable, sinister. Clots on the deck, spurts on the deckhouse, a slur of blood on the white steel rail above the wirework.

"You're quite a detective, Sheldon," said Krieg. "Smart work."

"I just happened to be the first to see it," said the steward. "I felt responsible for what happened to the young

lady. I didn't think it would have murder tied up in it."

"Murder?" said Burthwaite. "You think it's murder?"

The staff captain came toward them.

"There's another man missing," he said, his voice dry and precise and official. "Butler. He's a junior quartermaster—or was. A steady lad. No question about something having happened to him. He wasn't the skylarking kind. And he's gone. He was on deck watch."

"I found these blood stains, captain," said Sheldon.

"The lad's been killed," he said. "And not by any damned ghost, either. Someone on board has done this. It's a nasty business."

"We'll handle it," said Burthwaite. "Have the ship searched. Get the captain up."

"I've called him already," said the mate.

"What would this Butler have been doing abaft the funnel on this deck?" demanded Burthwaite.

"Nothing, sir," replied the mate. "He would only have come aft if he saw something going on he didn't think was right. Then he might interfere. It looks as if he did, to his cost."

"He may be aboard," said Krieg. "If he's still alive we can question him."

"There's the blood mark on the rail," put in Sheldon, the steward. "Two of them. One looks as if he might have grabbed at it, and lost his grip."

They gazed at the rushing sea, in shadow from the hull. Beyond the umbra it ran in glittering ranks. They heard the sound of the water's run along the ship, the hiss of the wake. But the sea held its secret.

IT was Francine's custom when aboard to serve her mistress's breakfast in bed, receiving the tray he steward, with its selected contents.

This morning little had been ordered. Sheldon brought it in. To Francine's astonishment he spoke to her in French that was fluent and accurate.

"I would like to see your mistress," he said. "I am a friend. I have a letter to her concerning me from a very dear friend of hers. You also are her friends and perhaps you may guess his name."

"You mean M'sieur Q. . ." asked Francine. Her Latin heart rejoiced in romance, in mystery. Also she liked the looks of this new steward.

"M'sieur John Carlin Quincy, the Second, none other," replied Sheldon in continental manner. "I will trust you with the letter to deliver to m'selle and see if she will see me."

Gallantly he kissed the hand that Francine extended for the sealed envelope. It was not the hand a sculptor would have chosen but it was an honest hand and the salute was genuine.

Mary Atchison read the enclosure and health seemed to flow into her at sight of the dear, familiar writing, the beloved signature, the brief but glowing phrases. They belonged with the sunshine that flowed in through the porthole where that hideous face had peered the night before.

Darling:

This is Charles Sheldon. He is a friend of mine, first of all, and next, though perhaps the most important, he is an investigator. A detective, he would call himself, but it is a term that does not fit him in its usual comprehension. He was at college with me, he is a fraternity brother and we both got our letters on the football team. I went to him as to no one else and he threw aside business to look after you. I had nothing

very definite to give him save that I believe I have reason to think you in grave danger, even aboard your uncle and guardian's yacht. Sheldon agrees with me. We have managed, rather he has managed, in a way he has, to get a berth as steward on the Albatross. If and when he feels it necessary he will get in touch with you. Trust him absolutely. I have trusted him with you, and I would not do that lightly. I love you, always and all ways,

John.

"Show him in," she said to Francine. "You are a friend," she said as Sheldon entered. "I think I need one."

Sheldon the steward nodded gravely. "You don't mind if I ask you some questions?" he asked. "Nor if I don't explain them. I may be wrong. John Quincy may be wrong and we would be sorry if our mistakes made trouble, but I have seen enough since I signed on as one of the crew to confirm Quincy's fears and some of his suspicions."

He studied her closely. He had many times listened to Quincy's eulogies of his sweetheart, his description of her as vibrant with health, a good sport, an athlete, not afraid of anything. She was afraid now, Sheldon saw plainly enough. He had studied many branches of art and science to qualify himself for his chosen profession, that embraced the thrill of adventure and the solution of mystery. He knew medicine and psychology. Something had happened in this girl that had eroded the barrier between her conscious and subconscious functioning. It was a dangerous condition but he could see plenty of traces of a once splendid woman. Her spirit was still brave but it was in rétreat. He would have to be careful.

"There is no question that you are in danger," he said. "I was not sure, I am not sure yet, what forms it may take. That is why I gave you the pistol."

"Doctor Krieg thought, that is he looked at me, as if he thought I might mean to—to kill myself with it," she said.

Sheldon grinned at her. The change for the better she had experienced with Quincy's note was still working like a leaven in her.

"You're not contemplating anything like that, are you?" he asked, still smiling.

She shook her head. "No. I have been melancholy, I have felt sometimes as if life was not worth living but I wouldn't take my own."

Sheldon nodded. She was that sort. Instinct would hold her back from suicide unless her mind actually broke down. She was still sound but she was like an engine with poor fuel, with the wrong kind of lubricant and poor radiation.

Now, with someone standing by, a friend of her lover, she would be more resistant against outside malign influence but that did not remove her from deadly peril.

"That face you saw, last night," he said. "Of course there was nothing supernatural about it. We found definite traces of the person who was masquerading in such fashion. But I believe the apparition was deliberately staged to upset you. The superstitious sailors talk about such things, naturally. The apparition appeared two or three times before you came aboard, while the yacht was at its moorings, being made ready for sea. That was all part of the climax. When Doctor Krieg spoke to the stewards, with the valets and maids, warning them

against the gossip, he may have thought he laid that fake phantom, but it was certain to be talked about, certain that Francine, your own maid, essentially sensitive to such tales of apparitions with her Breton blood, would repeat it to you. Other maids probably chattered but Francine was a sure bet."

"What do you mean by a sure bet?" asked the girl. "How can I be in danger on my uncle's own yacht? Why should I be subjected to any attack?"

"I can't answer all that, Miss Atchison," said Sheldon gravely. "That is why I am here—to find out—to prevent. Quincy felt he had justification in his fears for you. When he told me what he knew, what he imagined, I felt even more strongly than he did that there was cause and motive in existence. We may be wrong as to the source and it would be a grave mistake to decide without proof but, since I joined the Albatross I have seen that justification increased. I mean by a 'sure bet' that I think that phantom face was rigged up, the tale and appearance deliberately started with the final idea of shattering your health."

She was not strong enough to be told about the second missing man, the telltale blood stains, he decided. He had to be vague, to count upon what he could establish of personal confidence in himself, backed by Quincy's introduction and endorsement.

"I am sorry to be vague," he went on, "but I shall be on the lookout night and day. Meanwhile, although it was your uncle's request that nothing be said, it has leaked out inevitably that you saw the phantom last night; also that it shocked you terribly. There is always a grapevine telegraph on board a ship that runs from stokehole to pantry, from forecastle to bridge. There will be more gossip among the maids. You will find your guests ready to offer you condolences, to sympathize with your nervousness.

"I want you to make light of it, even if you have to fib your doctor a bit how you feel. Bravery and confidence will bring your pulses up and fool the best physician. Not really fool him, at that, because the mind is the master. Be brave and cheerful and you will be sanguine, which means healthy. So, even if Doctor Krieg suggests your resting in seclusion, I should suggest your coming out among your friends if you feel you can do it, with a good front."

She laughed. It was the first time she had laughed in weeks, and she said so.

"You see, I am better already. I can take it on the chin. Doctor Krieg is very careful of me but I don't think he'll be very angry if I break orders. He'll be too glad to see me feeling so well."

"Without question," said Sheldon. "But please do not tell him, do not tell anyone, why. About my real position here, about the note I brought you. It might be resented and my position as your guard destroyed.

She nodded. "Did you send me the note, too?" she asked.

"No. Where is it?"

She showed him the torn fragments she had preserved. He asked her to repeat the contents as well as she remembered them and she did so.

"I'd like to have these," he said. "Have you told anyone else about it?"

"Nobody. I thought of showing it to uncle and then I decided not to bother him. He despises anonymous letters."

"That's fine. I must be going. Trust me, Miss Quincy. I shall be standing by."

She gave him her hand. It was no longer cold. The warm blood of youth pulsed through it and her eyes shone, her head was erect.

"Good girl!" he said. "Quincy told me he was the luckiest man in the world. I discounted that statement at the time. I withdraw the reservation."

CHAPTER FOUR

The Fight on the Deck

HIS own eyes were grave and thoughtful when he went out, he carried out his many duties with a courtesy that offset any little detail of service he overlooked. He made a good steward. The women guests watched him approvingly; the maids cocked their chins and rolled their eyes at him, in vain. He told the latter, quite mendaciously, that he was a recent widower and, while they would have liked to console him, they could appreciate his present attitude.

He did not have much leisure until the interval between luncheon and tea but the problem he was there to solve worked like a steady ferment in his subconscious. All the time he observed, filed, made little deductions, picking up pieces of a jigsaw puzzle that presently he would fit together in a pattern. Such solutions came swiftly once the start was made, especially when the final picture began to resemble what he thought it would.

His own situation was far from sure. If Burthwaite even suspected that his new steward was a detective, which, to Burthwaite, was the same as a spy, that imperious gentleman would be quite capable of setting Sheldon adrift on a pontoon, if he didn't have him thrown overboard. Burthwaite was, as Quincy, Senior said, a good deal of a pirate, a modern buccaneer of Wall Street, even as Captain Kidd had been of the high seas.

They were well off shore. The weather was warm and the Atlantic shore line was lost in haze. They sheared fast through the long ground-swells. Sheldon got the news of their run and speed in the stewards' room, where the junior officers foregathered for an extra snack or a surreptitious tot of grog. Roughly speaking, it was a thousand miles from New York to the Bahamas. They were reeling this off steadily at thirty knots. They should be off Great Abaco by midnight, it was said, if the weather held and the wind did not head them.

By the course they were making they were not going to touch at Nassau. Cuba was eliminated because of the revolution brewing there. It was generally understood they would make for the Windward Islands but the captain was close-mouthed about his orders.

There was a lot of quiet, sober talk about the missing quartermaster, Butler. His disappearance, the suggestion of murder, quieted the usual gossip, gave it a somber turn. The phantom face was mentioned but not as anything supernatural. The wet footprints had dried, the blood had been scraped from rail and planks and removed from the steel side of the deckhouse by order of Burthwaite, but their significance remained.

It was perhaps a trifle high handed of Burthwaite to remove that evidence, but this was his yacht and he was responsible for his orders. Naturally he did not want any curious guests to discover the sanguinary blotches. They knew nothing of the missing man, and they chatted cheerily. At the request of Doctor Krieg, ingratiating and popular, they said nothing to Mary Atchison about the hideous face at her porthole. Krieg shook a half-playful finger at her once in a while for disobeying his orders but there was no question as to her welfare, body and spirit.

As Sheldon had prophesied, the grapevine telegraph had been at work. But, not having seen the phantom themselves, they were disposed to regard it as hallucination on 'dear Mary's' part. Krieg did not discourage the idea. He wanted it to die down. As for the murder, if it was a murder, that was a thing so serious that, for once, those who knew about it respected the order to keep it to themselves. It did not get aft among the passengers. A few were surprised that Burthwaite did not head for Nassau to report it to the police but, after all, he was an American, and why should he go to British authorities—or turn back from his trip, for the sake of a missing seaman? Sailors had been lost at sea before. It went down in the log to be when the voyage ended.

The radio sputtered a good deal, sending and receiving. It was supposed the matter had been reported, but both Sparks and his junior were to all intents and purposes dumb. To talk would mean the loss of their jobs. Also Burthwaite invariably sent everything in code to his own offices and it was said that nothing, not even the light messages of some lady guest, went out, or came in, without his personal supervision.

Every now and then a messenger took him a little batch of messages, outgoing or incoming, the former filed for his approval, the latter for his perusal. Sometimes he chuckled grimly. Some were in a code not his own and those he set aside and destroyed if he failed to interpret them. They were from his own particular guests and they had to do with stocks and bonds. They might play but Burthwaite was dealing the cards and if he dealt off the bottom now and then, his friends were not above playing tricks. All was fair on the Exchange, was their motto. Burthwaite was the Buffalo Bull but they were curly wolves. He had a deal to propose to them which he had not yet broached. They meant to make sure he did not get all the grease out of that goose while they plucked it.

Every hour their position, checked by revolutions and the log, was sent to an address in New Orleans, a branch of certain New York brokers whose firm name did not include that of Burthwaite though he was a hidden, if not silent, partner in the concern.

AT noon on the second day a big amphibian was being overhauled by a flyer named Traveau. He gave reporters no satisfaction as to what he was up to. He had clearance papers that covered a wide territory to the south. They give planes a lot of latitude these days that may later be denied. Mystery as to a destination is not necessary. One may always be forced down. Which is an excellent reason why airships are, so far, much superior for illicit and contraband purposes to ships that sail or steam on charted seas.

There was one room on the Albatross fitted with a blackboard and electric connections that steadily gave out, through radio, the prices on Exchange and Curb Market. There were certain passengers of Burthwaite's who spent most of their time lolling there, watching the quotations, sipping highballs and smoking strong cigars. A steward was in attendance besides the board tender. Occasionally Burthwaite looked in with a chuckle at some turn in the tide of finance. There was not much to smile at—unless you were a Buffalo Bull. Despite all presidential boostings that tide was ebbing steadily. Now

and then there was a ripple but it always subsided. Pools and mergers failed to stem its subsidence. Burthwaite appeared confident.

"Wait a bit, gentlemen," he told them. "It's not quite ripe."

"If it ain't ripe now it'll soon be rotten," said one member of the quartet he had invited on the cruise—and for a certain coup he had not yet revealed.

They had little time to lose and they might gain much if Burthwaite had a killing on and needed them to complete it. They were sure he was short of cash. They had marveled he had not gone under in the last slump, carrying what they knew he did. The man was a marvel, with unexpected and unknown resources. They had thought they knew just how much he had, in negotiable securities and cash, and he had fooled them. They had still remained his friends, fortunately, and now he wanted to pool their resources in a sure thing.

They were a shark-eyed quartet. Curly wolves they might be, eager to drag down any quarry, but their eyes were the eyes of sharks. They were clever manipulators — jugglers — of stocks and bonds. The industries represented meant nothing to them; they were not patriotic. They were out for marrow and if it had to come from dead men's bones it was just as nutritious.

Sheldon served them for a while and watched them, avaricious, furtive, watching each other to see how the flashing change of prices might affect. They did not discover much. They had poker faces, all of them. But they did not trust in anyone, much less the God on the dollar's motto. If they were in anything together it would have to be not only to their mutual advantage but hedged about with infinite precautions. It took a past master like the Buffalo Bull himself to get them in a deal and handle it.

At last he got in his own bunk, the only steward but one off present duty. It was a cabin for four. The other snored and Sheldon went to work on the torn-up scraps of the note.

It was not so much warning as menace to a nervous girl, he told himself. But it was a clue—a real clue. The ink was glossy-black in some lights but, in others, it showed a certain iridescence. Only chemical tests could be definite but there were not many inks that would show that rainbow tint when the pasted-up sheet was slanted. He was sure the note was part of the plan to upset Mary Atchison's troubled nerves—together with the tale of the phantom. The face might appear again; he thought it would.

He had no fear, now he had talked with her, that she would attempt suicide but he fancied the originator of this devilish plan might have counted on it —and counted on another thing. Whoever he, or they, were, they meant to erase her.

Given out—and shown—that her health had broken down, that her nerves were shattered, and then her disappearance would be sufficient. She might be drugged, through the same means that had found entrance to her chamber and left the note, then dropped overboard. If the motive were sufficient that would not be anything extraordinary these days. There would have been ample indications of a troubled and depressed mind, cause for suicide. Her friends and relatives would accept it. For lack of evidence, so would the law.

But, Sheldon, told himself grimly, as he folded up the reconstructed note, there would be other evidence. He himself had placed the pistol on the bed by using his steward's master key to the suite while Francine gossiped with the maids after he had slipped away from the meeting. It would be interesting to find out who had been able to get a key to the bedroom door into the little hall. Mary Atchison could bolt the one between her sleeping room and her dressing room.

He was going carefully. He could not lightly accuse the men he believed responsible. He had to have definite proof first. Hunches were all right. usually the inevitable conclusions of observation coupled with a faculty for detection—but in this game he knew he was combating brains perhaps more brilliant than his own, one brain at least that calculated far in advance.

One thing he knew, unless all his deductions were wrong. The sudden convalescence of Mary Atchison, her apparent return to normal—or close to normal—was going to upset here enemies. They would try to reduce that condition. Sheldon did not think they would actually murder her. They meant to make away with her for their own purposes, perhaps their own safety, as he set down the problem; but they would not dare to kill, except as a last resort.

Butler had been killed—because he interfered with their maneuvers.

Mary Atchison was to be eliminated because she interfered with their welfare. Because she threatened that welfare.

He wondered whether they would try to use the phantom face again. He thought so. And he hoped so. This time he would be closer at hand.

THE Albatross was off the Bahamas; the night was clear. There was no wind but the air held the balm of the tropics, hints of perfumed flowers and waving palms. There was seafire in the wake and about the stem, along the run. Stars burned in a sky of purple velvet and were mirrored here and there in the heave of the sea of liquid ebony. Land was far off, to starboard, low islands covered with verdure. Here Columbus had made shore and uncovered fame. There was a glamor about the scene but the passengers barely noticed it, the crew was used to it.

They followed sailing instructions, their duties were automatic, or else they slept. Music played; couples danced. Others played the inevitable game of contract. Burthwaite and his friends bluffed each other at poker. Mary Atchison was with her guests. She had a talisman tucked into the bosom of her dress that was a charm against all evil —the note from her lover. Now and then she caught sight of Sheldon, the steward, moving deftly here and there, and she felt strong against all trouble.

Doctor Krieg smiled at her approvingly, but warned her not to overexert herself. "I want you to break this up early," he said.

"I can't be rude."

"Of course not. But you are so much improved I don't want to have any setback."

At a little time after two bells the electrics paled, flickered, went out, returned to dull red glows and finally expired. Servants brought temporary lights, candles and a lamp or two. A dynamo had burned out something or other. Burthwaite cursed the engineer but repairs were uncertain. The guests drifted off to bed. A couple or two lingered but, by four bells—two o'clock —they had all turned in. There was a battery light in the binnacle. The Albatross held its course.

Once more Mary Atchison woke with a start. Her nerves were still jumpy. An icy finger seemed tracing out her backbone and her heart raced once again

as she saw the porthole illumined with a faint greenish glow.

Then there came the face, the drowned, hideous face, with those flaming, ghostly orbs. The hair like weed, the avid awful mouth, the——

It was gone. It had disappeared as if the wraith had been snatched away, rather than dissolved! It was gone! Gone!

And her terror seemed to evaporate. Her reason ruled. Her coordination still failed her but she was not afraid. Someone had come to her rescue— Sheldon. John Quincy's friend.

Her womanly intuition had been right. Sheldon had been lying flat on top the deckhouse for over an hour, dressed in black pajamas, black socks, black sneakers and with a black beret over his light hair—waiting for the phantom. The failure of the lights had been more than purely accidental, he fancied. It had driven the guests to their beds whereas otherwise they would have lingered until dawn. It looked like stage craft and he was prepared to play his part.

That was far from a simple role. He might discover and even denounce but unless he did that so definitely as to banish all doubt in the presence of many witnesses, he would be discredited, made a fool of. He could not get his proofs in the order he desired, he might not be able to get them—some of them—at all. He was working alone on a boat run by an autocrat who would naturally resent any such interference. And he was pitted against criminals of no mean order—clever, resourceful, imaginative and unscrupulous.

His pulse beats merged into seconds, seconds into interminable minutes.

He had left a dummy in his bunk, trusting to the sleepiness of the other man off watch. He had to be back there by eight bells—four o'clock—before dawn, before the stewards' watch changed.

He hugged the undercurve of a pontoon. It was almost impossible for anyone on deck to see him but he was not as close to the edge of the roof as he would have liked. He strained his ears, knowing well that the man who played the phantom would be silent.

Then he fancied he heard the slight click of a door.

He rolled over, clinging to a lifeline on the pontoon.

There was a dark form beneath him. It stooped, stood upright. Its face glowed with weird light as it was slowly upraised. Then came tapping on porthole glass. The frightful countenance gazed through the circular window and Sheldon launched himself, twisting as he went, twining his legs about the phantom's very real and muscular waist and legs, seeking to get a half Nelson on the marauder.

He would have got it had not the other suddenly displayed, for all the surprise of the attack, a defense that came out of gymnasium or professional quarters. The man knew the parry and applied it. They went to the deck together and Sheldon found himself in a toehold that tortured him to desperation. He was not a wrestler, rather a boxer, as amateur athletics went, but he snaked and twisted free and they rose together.

Now he could see the hideous face and he swung at it, parrying a blow off his elbow. His own went to the mark but was muffled and though the other staggered he was not badly hurt. Sheldon brought up a jab from the hip with his right and felt it meet and jar with the well-muscled but lean ribs of a man in good training. He needed a gun for this sort of job but dared not use one.

Neither did the other man. It had to be a silent scuffle, silent as it was unexpected on the part of the one with the appalling features. Sheldon tried to close with him. He gripped the cloth of his garment in the fingers of his left hand, groped for and found a belt. But the other was no tyro. He gave ground and then, suddenly, a hand shot for Sheldon's face. A thumb sought for his eyeball to dislodge it and a knee forged into his groin with a stab of red-hot agony. It was a foul blow and it could not be withstood.

CHAPTER FIVE

The Showdown

SHELDON went down to the deck, writhing, blind with torment, still seeking for an adversary who had fled. He got to his feet with difficulty. In his hand he still gripped a shape of cloth that gleamed in the darkness that was beginning to lessen as the first hint of a gray false dawn showed out at sea.

It was a mask, cleverly painted and contrived, with phosphorescent paint and false eyes of blown green glass in which radium glowed with a light that looked unreal, supernatural. The eyes were misplaced, high in the form of papier-miché. Beneath them there were holes through which the wearer might see. The thing was hideous in its fixed grin, its streaming strands of hair, the simulacrum of a face whose owner was long drowned.

As Sheldon got to his feet the night was like a shaken curtain above the sea where spangled stars were quivering, paling. It was close to eight bells. He must get back to his berth unless he was prepared to strike and before that he must produce the man who had worn this falseface. He was sure he knew who it was but he must have proof. He might not be given the chance to obtain it if he were not on hand as steward. He might be charged himself with the impersonation.

His groin throbbed and he fought back the weakness and the pain. He leaned against the housing and a port opened close to his head. In the faintly increasing light he saw it was the face of Mary Atchison in the opening. A pallid face but devoid of fear, resolute, the features of one who had conquered dread.

"Get back," he said. "This is Sheldon. I've unmasked the phantom. I'll soon——"

He stopped. They both listened to the drone of an engine, up in the sky, throbbing with regular resonance in the still morning air. Sheldon looked up and saw the shape of a large amphibian circling above them. He heard the amplified tones of a voice coming through a loud-speaker.

"Albatross. Slow down. Turn Burthwaite out. Tell him it's Mason, with Traveau."

Traveau. That named evoked recollection, Mason only vaguely so. But the voice was imperative and confident. Not many men spoke to or concerning Burthwaite without using some prefix.

"Go turn him out or we'll swamp you."

Something fell from the big plane, hurtling to the sea, exploding in a geyser of water and pale flame. It was a bomb.

"Next one we'll drop on your funnel," said the magna vox. "It's up to you."

Sheldon waved the girl back, called to her to close the port. This was something he had not counted on.

The Albatross was slowing down with reversed engines. Men were showing on deck. The amphibian swooped lower, barely two hundred feet above the deck as Burthwaite came storming out in his brocaded robe. He had a megaphone he had snatched in his hand and he bellowed through it.

"What's the idea of this, Mason? What do you mean by it?"

"Tell you when I come aboard. We got two quickfires. We can spray you plenty, aside from the bombs. Now line up your pals, likewise your lady guests, and put off a boat. No funny business or we'll blow it into splinters."

Sheldon saw Burthwaite stand there like a man at whom kindly Jove has suddenly flung a thunderbolt. The staff-captain came on deck and Burthwaite yelled at him to put off a boat. He glimpsed another steward and told him to arouse his personal guests, Chapman, Klein, Edwards and Macy. There was hardly need for this. The amphibian dropped another charge close by and the dull roar of it awakened everyone that the accompanying plunge and rocking of the yacht did not arouse.

The four financiers emerged sleepily in more or less fantastic garments, demanding to know what was wrong.

"I don't know," rapped Burthwaite. "Something's in the wind."

THEY clustered round him, suspicious and protesting. Other guests showed up with wraps against the chill of morning. The big plane had lit upon its pontoons like a great bird, dark against the sun which had not yet wheeled over the horizon, but showed the increasing light of its imminent rise.

There came the swift tat-a-tat-a-tat of two machine guns, mounted fore and aft, not aimed at the bow now making for it, but seemingly two trial bursts of flame and lead in dramatic warning.

They waited, the Albatross lifting to the heave with stilled engines, while the boat came back with two passengers in the stern. These were the men called Mason and Slugger who had watched the yacht depart from Huntingdon Harbor.

Sheldon, swiftly changing into shore clothes, emerged from his quarters.

The captain proper was in charge and he glared at Sheldon. "What in hell are you doing up here?" he challenged.

"Know something about this, I think," said Sheldon, though he was not too sure. But he showed a star that made the captain give him audience.

"I've got one gun," said Sheldon. "I know where I can get another. How about you?"

"I've got one," said the captain, "but I don't know——"

"You will in a minute," said Sheldon. "Better stand by."

The captain trailed him down to the deck. Sheldon sought out Mary.

"It looks like a showdown," he said. "Where's that gun I gave you?"

"I can get it."

"Do that," he said.

The boat was coming to where they had rigged the gangway and Sheldon slid into the stateroom marked E, the quarters of Doctor Krieg. He was there only a few seconds.

The two men came over the rail, Mason the hawk-faced, Slugger with his broken nose and cauliflower ears.

"Now then," said Burthwaite, "what's this? Are you drunk?"

"Not a bit. I'm not taking orders from you any more, Burthwaite. You're washed up, so far as I'm concerned. I'm not wasting much time on you either. You hired me to head you off, like we've done, and take you and these four gents—they look like the four you mentioned—Chapman, Klein, Macy and Edwards—away with you. Kidnap you, hold you for ransom. It was a fake, so far as you were concerned. We were to get a cut on what the rest dug up. You were broke, you said, and it seems that's about right. But so are these gents.

"We got some inside information that beats even yours, Burthwaite, sometimes. We need it in our business. These four guys are all indicted by the State Legislature Commission on Fraudulence. Bum banks and what not. They know. You might be mixed up in it yourself, Burthwaite. The point is all the money they can raise personally is tied up. All the jack their friends—if they got any left —could dig up they'll need for bail. They ain't worth a dollar a dozen to us but we hate to work for nothing so we'll collect ours by a public donation from your passengers, cash and jewels."

They both stood at the head of the gangway and their guns were out, menacing. Their faces were hard and ugly. Mason swung his automatic.

"Come on," he snarled. "We can't stay here all day. Line up. You— where are you going?"

"Thought I'd send a radio," said Sheldon quietly. "Why?"

The utter insolence of his reply made Mason gasp. It checked him for a second and it held the slower Slugger stupefied.

THEN Mason's automatic spat fire. The bullet left a smear of lead against the deckhouse as it sang against the steel with a dull note. Mason went staggering back to the rail where it was open to the gangway, a slug from Sheldon's weapon in his left shoulder, toppling into the boat. The captain shoved through with his weapon and Slugger, growling like a bear, knocked it down and fired in return. He got the missile in his foot and his own went skyward as Sheldon shattered his elbow.

The amphibian rose and fell on the surge. They had expected to carry off five passengers in their kidnaping stunt. And Traveau, who must have heard the shots come down the wind, made up his mind it was a good time to leave.

"Got those two men, captain," said Sheldon. "Better go about and make for New York. I'll send that radio presently. Get your boat in."

"And who the devil do you think you are and what the devil do you mean by giving orders on my boat?" demanded Burthwaite. He did not recognize his steward out of uniform.

"Name's Sheldon," said the detective. "You'll know soon enough. I'll see you later. I want to talk with Doctor Krieg first—then you. It was too bad Mason gave you away. He'll help my case against you though I've a strong notion Krieg will come across."

Sheldon turned to Mary Atchison who was asking what he meant. "I'm sorry," he said. "It can't be helped. Krieg, come here."

The popular doctor had lost all his suavity. He advanced slowly, his face set, compelled by Sheldon's weapon.

"Krieg," said Sheldon. "I've got your record, just as Burthwaite got it and held it over you. I looked you up on the request of John Quincy, Junior to find out just what sort of physician had been called in to take care of her. You could be held for malpractice on this case, aside from the practice you handled in New York, which Burthwaite knew and chose to overlook. It was you who used the disappearance of Thompson to bring up the story of his ghost, you who wore a mask to play phantom and frighten Miss Atchison into insanity, you who killed young Butler. You sent Miss Atchison a frightening note and foolishly used the special copying ink in your fountain pen, which I have. It was you—"

"That's enough," said Krieg. "It

was I. But Burthwaite, the devil, made me do it, forced me to do it. He wanted his niece out of the way because he had used all her money to save his own smash-up and could not produce it when she comes of age. He barely saved himself. He planned to have his friends held for ransom to give him more money—though I did not know of that. He promised me a quarter of a million dollars—they would have paid it—a quarter of a million dollars—or the penitentiary."

"Or the chair," said Sheldon.

"Or the chair. You are clever, Mister Detective, but you have overlooked one thing. I can't swim."

With a bound he leaped to the rail and plunged like a plummet into the sea. They got ready for it. The boat cast off. But, save for a few bubbles that was the end of Krieg.

They had Mason and Slugger. Traveau was away but the radio could trace him down. Sheldon turned on Burthwaite who stood with surly defiance, his four associates regarding him as if he were poison. Krieg was gone but Mason would testify against him. He had no resources. He looked gloomily at the sea—then at Sheldon's gun. He shrugged his shoulders.

"I'm going to my cabin," he said.

"I'll go with you," said Sheldon.

He was conscious of Mary Atchison's pitiful gaze following her uncle, discredited and disarmed of his chief weapon, money. Two days and she would be comforted in her lover's arms. Young Quincy had plenty and Sheldon was not too sorry for her.

As for himself—it had been an interesting case. He had bluffed Krieg a bit. But—once the pattern began to show, it swiftly established itself. Krieg had tossed up his hand, knowing it was a losing one.

Hell's Pay Check

by

Frederick Nebel

Author of "Death Alley," etc.

It was only an oblong strip of paper but it had been drawn at the point of a gun, endorsed in blood. Detective Cardigan knew that no man must cash it, that he must follow it to Death's clearing-house, cancel it with a pen dipped in flaming lead.

"I'm hit!" Joe gasped, and
fell over a flower bed,
cursing.

CHAPTER ONE

Death on Arrival

THE change in the tune of the train
wheels roused Cardigan. He used
a broad palm to wipe steam from
the rain-wet coach window. The train
was crossing the Wabash River. Beyond were the lights of the city.

Cardigan bent over, dropped a magazine into an open grip, started to close
it. On second thought, he drew out a
38 revolver and slipped it into his hip
pocket; closed, locked the grip.

He rose, a big, shaggy-headed man

with a burry outdoor look, shrugged into a wrinkled topcoat, put on a faded
fedora that had seen better days. He
lugged his bag to the nearest vestibule.
The locomotive's bell gonged more re-
sonantly as the train pulled into the station.

Cardigan swung down to the platform, shook his head at a barging porter,
tramped heavy-footed through the
waiting room. He dwarfed an aver-
age-sized man. His shoulders rocked.
He slapped open a door with the flat
of his hand, felt a gust of rain and raw
fall wind. He moved along slowly,
looking at the license plates of parked

cars. Then he stopped before a large black sedan and was regarding the windshield curiously when the front door opened and a man in a chauffeur's cap stepped out.

"Mr. Cardigan?"

"Yeah."

The chauffeur saluted, pivoted and opened the rear door. He took Cardigan's bag, and Cardigan climbed in. The bag landed after him. The chauffeur climbed in front, started the motor, clicked into gear.

Cardigan leaned back, rolled a fresh cigar between his lips, nibbled off the tip, spat it through an open window. He lit up and watched wet buildings flash past. The car turned into the main drag, where trolley bells clanged, auto horns honked, and red neon lights scrawled advertisements in the rainy dark.

"Wet night," said the chauffeur.

"Lousy."

"Train was on time, though."

"Yeah. How far out is this place?"

"It ain't far. Say, you're that private dick made such a haul out in St. Louis in the summer, ain't you?"

"Better keep your eyes on the road," Cardigan said.

They shot through a railroad underpass, rolled through a tatterdemalion part of the city. The chauffeur's ears stuck out from his head. He kept wiping sweat from the inside of the windshield. Cardigan was uninterested in the scenery. He was rather fascinated by the way the chauffeur's ears stuck out.

"Much further?" he asked.

"It ain't far," the chauffeur said.

Cardigan squinted at the back of his head, took two long, ruminative puffs. "Stop at the next cigar store. I want to get some pipe tobacco."

"Mr. Edwards'll have plenty."

"That's all right. I said I want to get some pipe tobacco."

"All right, then, all right."

A minute later the chauffeur pulled up to the curb and Cardigan opened the door, stepped out and strode into a cigar store. The windows were opaque with steam. Cardigan slipped into a telephone booth, looked at a yellow slip of paper, made a call. Half a minute later he stepped out, picked up a tin of tobacco and went outside.

"I'll ride in front," he said. "Lucky he had my brand."

"I don't smoke a pipe," the chauffeur said, and rolled the car from the curb.

They rode in silence for a few minutes. Then Cardigan drew his gun and pressed it against the chauffeur's ribs.

"Now where the hell are you really going?" he said.

"Hey, what the—"

"Cut it out, you fat-head! Keep your hands on that wheel and don't try handing me a line."

The chauffeur was gripping the wheel hard with both hands. He didn't look at Cardigan. He stared intently through the windshield, his body tense, his shoulders hunched.

"Take the first right-hand turn," Cardigan said. "Go around the block and back to the city."

"Cripes, chief—"

"Lay off, lame-brain—lay off. The next time you try to act like a chauffeur—act like one. You've been a heel so long that your heel-conscious." He jabbed his gun hard against the man's ribs, snapped, "Turn right!"

The man heaved on the wheel. The car skidded on the wet pavements, grazed a tree, slewed badly but held its balance. Behind, on the main street they had left, brakes ground and tires screeched. Cardigan looked back and saw a curtained touring car skidding to a stop.

"Step on!" Cardigan muttered.

"Geeze——"

"Step on it!"

The sedan gathered speed. Looking back, Cardigan saw the touring car in reverse. Then he saw it swing into the side street. The sedan swung right again, skidding, and the man at the wheel groaned and cursed.

"Right at the next," Cardigan said, "and back to the main drag."

"What a sweet spot you put me in!"

"I'm glad of that."

"They'll think I'm two-timin'!"

"Swell!"

The chauffeur snarled, "You ain't sittin' so pretty yourself!"

The rear end slewed wildly as they took the next right. The rear left wheel struck the opposite curb. The car heaved, slammed back to all fours. The chauffeur threw out the clutch, raced the motor to keep it from stalling, meshed gears again savagely and skidded on the get-away.

The beams of the touring's headlights sparkled on the rain-beaded rear window of the sedan. The chauffeur sank deep in the seat, gritting his teeth, gripping the wheel low. Cardigan twisted around and hunched down on the floor.

A gun banged in the wet dark. The rear window fell out with a crash. A hole appeared in the center of the non-shatterable windshield, with spiderweb lines radiating.

"Look!" cried the chauffeur. "Look at that!"

"To hell with that! Step on it!"

"Me——I'm gonna stop!"

Cardigan trained his gun on the man. "You stop and I'll cave in your chest!"

"Oh, Gord! They think 'm two-timin'!"

He swung left into the main drag—

wildly. The wheels rasped on the wet pavement, screeched over trolley tracks. The big sedan shuddered. Miraculously it retained its balance, careened away, with the chauffeur's foot so hard on the throttle that the wheels lost traction momentarily and the rear end swung from left to right. Then the wheels gripped and the sedan shot ahead.

Another hole appeared magically in the windshield. The chauffeur choked and stared at it with horrified eyes. Then he saw a pole directly in front of him. He heaved at the wheel violently. The car slewed, skidded turned sidewise. It swung all the way around and across the tracks—and around again. The chauffeur gripped the wheel hard, his mouth open, his eyes frozen with horror.

The right front mudguard slammed against a pole. A window fell out of the car with a crash. Guns barked and lead ripped through the sedan's body. The chauffeur screamed and heaved up and another bullet knocked him down again. The touring car roared past.

Cardigan pushed open the door, pawed glass splinters from his face. He looked once at the chauffeur's head. Another look was unnecessary. He hauled his bag out of the back of the car, ran with it across the sidewalk, back of a ramshackle house with boarded windows.

He ducked through a gap in a rotten board fence, screwing his feet into wet earth with each step to kill his footprints. He went along back of the fence, then paused in some tall grass, started to reach for his handkerchief; changed his mind. He tore off wet grass, made a pad of it, scrubbed his face and tossed the grass away. The grass and the rain were cold.

Cardigan shivered and threaded his way on back of other board fences, reached a side street and walked away from the main drag. A police siren moaned through the night. By dead reckoning Cardigan walked into the city limits, his coat collar up. The mirror of a chewing-gun slot-machine showed him that his face was not as bad as he had supposed. He sighed, whistled to himself and walked across the sidewalk into a taxi.

"Sixth and Diana," he said.

At Sixth he got off, walked north on Sixth, turned right at the first intersection and entered the Hotel Flatlands.

THE man sitting behind the enormous flat-topped desk of aged mahogany drew slowly on a large pipe shaped like an inverted question mark. He was massive himself, in keeping with the room's furnishings. Middle-aged, bald, except for offshoots of grayish hair above the ears, he had a large nose, a fighter's jaw, a broad, impressive forehead. Through black-ribboned pince-nez he gazed at the stocky youth who sat quivering on a straight-backed chair.

"Be calm, Otto," said the big man.

"Yes, sir. Y-yes, sir." The stocky youth's teeth chattered.

The big man frowned concernedly, rose and went to an eight-legged Boulle cabinet. From it he took decanter and glasses. He carried them to the desk.

"Not Napoleon, Otto, but brandy none the less."

He gave the youth a stiff jolt. Otto threw it over, choked, spluttered, grimaced. The big man chuckled, but the look in his eyes was not one of humor. Worry was there and a haunted light shimmering deep in the pupils.

Rain thrashed against the French windows.

Otto began stuttering. "I—I couldn't do anything, sir! They walked up to me—and I could see how their hands were in their pockets. They made me walk away from the car and they kept me in a touring car after one of them took my cap. They held guns against me there. Then after maybe an hour they told me to get out and walk away and say nothing. Our—your car was gone. Then they went too. I—I—"

"You could have done nothing else, Otto. Pull yourself together. That man Cardigan telephoned a second time and I thank God nothing serious has happened to him. He's on his way out."

The old negro in black livery came in. "Mr. Cardigan, suh."

A moment later Cardigan filled the doorway. He had left hat and coat with the butler and stood chafing his hands and staring keenly into the dimly lighted library. His shaggy hair stood out around his head.

The big man rose from behind the mahogany desk, held out his hand. Cardigan crossed the room shook it, peered levelly at the pince-nez.

"This is Otto Shreiner, my chauffeur," the big man said.

Otto rose and bowed. Cardigan took him in with a piercing look, said nothing.

The man with the pince-nez said, "Leave us, Otto."

Otto went out. The grandfather's clock ticked solemnly.

"Brandy, Mr. Cardigan?"

Cardigan said: "Thanks," poured himself a tot, sniffed the aroma, then drank it. He squinted one eye at the empty glass. "Well, Mr. Edwards, what's on your mind?"

"Sit down, won't you?"

Both sat down, facing each other across the flat-topped desk. The old man took off his pince-nez, leaned back.

"First," he said, "my name's not Edwards."

Cardigan, starting a fresh cigar, did not look up until he had it going smoothly. Then he spoke impersonally. "And then what?"

"I am the mayor of the city."

Cardigan maintained his impersonal stare. "Once I worked for a governor."

"I said 'Edwards', you know, on long distance because——" He shrugged and held his palms up, then fell into a moody silence.

Cardigan studied the red end of his fresh cigar and started speaking in a low, blunt voice. "All right, then, Mr. Holmes. I expected trouble, anyhow. I always expect trouble when a client telephones long distance, offers to pay all expenses, and adds——'details on arrival'. That's all O. K. by me. It's my business. But I'll be twice damned if I like to have trouble pile on my shoulder the minute I step off a train. I'll stand for almost anything, but I hate to get mixed up in a murder before I know what all the shooting's for."

That ripped Holmes out of his moody silence. He half rose, remained that way, exclaimed: "Murder!"

"And why I'm sitting here right now, Mr. Mayor, is one of the reasons why I believe in luck, a rabbit's foot and words like abracadabra."

Holmes fell back into the chair, gripping the sides. "But——you said——murder!"

"Don't take it so hard. It happens every day. Besides, the guy that got it was a hood anyhow. He was the nice little boy that played chauffeur and started to take me places. But I had a hunch the minute we started that something was wrong. So I phoned you from that cigar store and asked what your chauffeur looked like."

Holmes squared his jaw. "Did you have to kill him, by God?"

"Me? Hell, no. His pals did it. Trailing us in another car. When I made the hood turn around his pals got sore and opened the fireworks. I ducked out and kept my mouth shut. Did you report the theft of your car to the police?"

But Holmes was still thinking of murder. "Murder——murder," he repeated in a far-away voice.

"Did you?"

"Oh—— Well, Otto did. At the railway station."

"What did he tell them?"

"Just that three men had forced him away, held him prisoner for an hour, then let him go."

"Did he say he was waiting for me?"

"No."

"I've got to be sure. I've got to be sure because I want to know how I stand with the cops."

"Otto is in my confidence."

Cardigan got up and took a turn up and down the room. He stopped and looked at the mayor. "Where did you telephone me from, your office?"

"No——here. Right here."

"Any other phones in the house on this line?"

"No."

"All right. Then your wire was tapped. You'll hear about the murder soon enough, and your recovered car. Tell that chauffeur of yours to keep his mouth shut. You keep yours. Your enemies, whoever they are, know I'm working for you. That may be tough for you, but it's tougher for me. And now——" Cardigan sat down—— "why am I here?"

Holmes leaned forward. "To recover a check for twenty thousand dollars that I made payable to one Roberta Callahan, a notorious woman."

"In other words, if this check gets to

certain hands the notoriety won't do you any good."

"It will ruin me."

"You don't look like the kind of man would run around with a dangerous piece of fluff. Still, there was a governor——"

"I assure you I'm not," Holmes said with quiet dignity.

"Philanthropy?"

"Don't be droll. My son Edgar's a rather gay blade, and I did it for his sake. He became badly tangled with this woman and there was only one way out. I bought her off. I gave her my personal check for twenty thousand dollars two weeks ago. She immediately blossomed out in a new roadster, moved into a fine apartment——"

"You mean you want the cancelled check?"

"No——no. The check has not been through my bank. Don't you see? She cashed the check with someone—someone who is holding it against me. And I want that check."

"What makes you think some guy's holding it?"

Holmes tilted his jaw. "You know me—or of me, rather. The reform mayor. By Judas Priest, I am that! Edgar had to get himself involved with that—woman—and I, naturally being his father, had to get him out of it. Hence my check. And would a photograph of that check, printed in the daily tabloid here, help my reform platform? No—you needn't reply. The answer is obvious."

"Who would be holding that check?"

"Any number of persons. Our daily tabloid, the worst scandal sheet in the country. Or the Fusion crowd. Or Pat McHugh, the boss of the old party. Or somebody unknown to me who hopes to reap a fortune by passing it on to someone else. But there you

are. There's the situation. I blundered into this because I'm not as smart-alecky as a lot of people. I'm entirely innocent. You might say that my son would come to the fore and admit the check was written to clear him. But the rest could hoot that down—and they could buy off the woman. You see?"

Cardigan had slid way down into the chair. He regarded Holmes through narrow-lidded eyes. Suddenly he knew he liked Holmes, saw his position. Cardigan, no reformer himself but a hard party down to the core, had a habit of admiring qualities which he himself did not possess.

He sat up, taking out a notebook. "All right now, Mr. Holmes. Give me all the names of persons you suspect, and addresses if possible. I don't suppose you asked the woman who cashed the check for her."

"I dare not go near her. I will pay the person who holds that check now the amount written on it—but I must have it."

"You'll get it," Cardigan said.

CHAPTER TWO

Dough for a Dick

AT midnight Cardigan lay awake in the dark of his hotel room thinking. The rain had stopped. The sound of a crosstown trolley came up sharply out of the street.

Elections were a month hence, and old Mayor Holmes had things to think about. A reform platform is a ticklish thing to stand on. Wiseacres are always ready to accuse you of trying to kid the public, of playing the wolf in sheep's clothing. A confessed mountebank is always colorful, a good man rarely popular.

Thus thought Cardigan—until a

sound at the door dismissed philosophy and snapped him to the immediate present. He reached over to the little bed-table, got his hand on his revolver and sat up with the same motion. He heard the not quite silent movement of a key in the lock, a final click. Then a pause of utter silence. Then a vertical line of light appeared where the door opened on a crack. The door swung wide slowly, silently, and three men stood there. Two of them had guns drawn while the third moved into the background. One of the armed men reached in a hand seeking the light switch.

"That's far enough," Cardigan said. "One slight move out of any of you birds and the management'll be disturbed."

The two armed men remained motionless. Then one said: "Police, Cardigan."

"Show me."

The two men turned back their lapels.

Cardigan lowered his gun. "It's damned funny that I can't get a night's sleep without you guys prowling around here like correspondence-school detectives."

The horse-faced man snapped on the lights and said, "I'm Lieutenant Strout. This is Sergeant Blake. That's Massey, the house officer. You can go, Massey."

Strout closed the door in Massey's face. He put away his gun and Blake did likewise. Blake was a chubby-cheeked fat man with a sly, smiling face. Strout was tall, muddy-eyed.

"Let's see that rod," he said.

Cardigan reversed it and Strout took it by the butt. It was a jointless solid-frame gun. Strout smelled the barrel, examined the chamber, hefted it thoughtfully, tossed it back on the bed.

"That the only one you carry?"

"Yeah."

"Look around, Blake. There's his bag."

Blake ransacked Cardigan's handbag while Cardigan stuffed a pipe and watched him with mild amusement. Strout went through Cardigan's clothes, opened the dresser drawers. Blake left Cardigan's clothes on the floor beside the bag.

Strout sat down on a chair, struck a match on the veneered frame of the wooden bed, left a long scratch there.

"What were you doing in the mayor's car tonight, Cardigan?"

"Was I in the mayor's car?"

Strout spurted smoke through his nostrils. "Don't give me the run-around."

"Well, was I?"

"You got in it at the railroad station and the chauffeur was killed twenty minutes later on Prairie Avenue."

"Says who?"

"Says me."

"Get your proof, lieutenant, and we'll continue."

"Listen, you," Blake said with his sly smile. "We've heard a lot about you."

Strout went on. "It was a stolen car. You got in and the chauffeur wasn't the mayor's chauffeur. He was all shot up when we found him and the car was busted. He was cold meat. You rode with him."

Cardigan put his bare feet on the floor, buttoned up the coat of his blue cotton pajamas, pointed his pipe stem at Strout.

"Now I'll tell you what I did. I came out of the station looking for a taxi. A guy with a chauffeur's cap on said, 'Taxi!' like that. So I thought it was an independent, and as it was raining and the car was handy I climbed in. I told him to drive to the Hotel Flatlands. After a while I began to wonder where he was going. I asked him and he said where I told him. He began to look queer to me, but I wasn't looking for trouble. So I got out at a cigar store and went in and bought some tobacco. I thought it out. I left the store and walked away. I walked back to the city and came here."

Blake laughed in a shrill, mocking tone. "That's a fast one!"

"Well, what are you going to do about it?" Cardigan said.

"What are we going to do about it?" Blake cried. "Damn you, you can't—"

"Shut up, Jake," Strout said dully and kept looking at Cardigan with his muddy, humorless eyes. "This is damned funny, Cardigan," he went on. "You were in a stolen car and the guy that drove it was murdered."

"With my gun, I suppose."

"Not with that gun there, but that don't say you didn't have another."

Cardigan laughed harshly. "And they pin medals on you guys!"

Strout blew cigarette ash to the carpet. "What did you come here for?"

"To sleep." He swung back into bed, pulled the covers up to his neck.

"I mean the city," Strout said.

"To get the hell pestered out of me by a couple of dumb clucks wearing badges."

Strout looked sullen. "None of your lousy cheap wit, Cardigan! You may have a name where you come from for being a pretty swell dick, but names are all the same to me on a police blotter."

The bed covers erupted and Cardigan was sitting up again. "Any time a client engages me it's just the same as if he engaged a lawyer. He gets my confidence and the benefit of silence."

"But there's murder in this."

"Because a heel in a stolen car starts taking me for a ride, for some reason I don't know, and I'm wide awake enough to slip out of it; and because a little later the heel is murdered with a gun that isn't mine— Listen, Strout, why the hell should I get all hot and bothered and tell you the story of my life? Do you mean to sit there in those pants and tell me I ought to get gray worrying about it? Hot dog, what school did you go to?"

Blake snapped, "This mutt is looking for a bust in the puss!"

"Yeah, and I suppose you're going to do it. Any minute now I'm going to break into convulsions!"

Strout pushed Blake back and said to Cardigan: "You come down to headquarters tomorrow."

"Like hell I will. If you want me to come to headquarters go get a warrant for my arrest. You got a lame tip somewhere, Strout, and you're trying to make me believe that it's red-hot. At your age you should know better than try that one. It was whiskered before I was born."

Strout got up, put his bony fists on his hips, regarded Cardigan with sullen eyes. "You're bright as hell, ain't you?"

Cardigan lay back in bed, pulled up the covers. "On the way out, Strout, douse the lights and lock the door."

CARDIGAN was singing deep-throated under the shower next morning when the doorbell rang.

"Wait a minute," he yelled.

He stopped the shower, climbed out and rubbed himself down with a towel and then alcohol. He heaved into a bathrobe, kicked his feet into mules and tramped through the bedroom.

A little plump man with pomaded sandy hair and narrow shoulders stood holding a derby chest-high with both hands. Thirty-odd, he had a clerical ır. He wore expensive dark clothes. "May I come in?"

"You're a new one on me," Cardigan said, "but come on."

The man crossed the threshold and Cardigan's hands darted to his person, slapped pockets rapidly. Out of the man's left pocket he took a small, dark automatic, palmed it.

"You see," he said, "I never know," and kicked the door shut.

The little man smiled. "You're a man of parts, Mr. Cardigan. I'm sorry to have intruded so early. Be careful—the safety may not be closed."

"I find that out the minute I touch a gun. It is."

"Truly a man of parts."

Cardigan said: "Now get this. I just got up. I haven't eaten yet. I'm a lousy guy to do business with most of the time, but especially before breakfast. Cut out the drawing-room tricks and speak your piece."

"A most definite man also. My compliments." Smiling, the little man showed exquisite white teeth and crinkly red lips. "Very well. I shan't be long. Primo: what are you doing in the city?"

"Answer: none of your business."

"Of course, you are here working for the mayor."

"The words are in your mouth, not mine."

"Doubtless you came here to regain possession—for the mayor—of a piece of paper. Green, let us say. And watermarked. You know—those little wavy lines? Correct?"

"You make me sick," Cardigan growled. He extracted six 25 calibre shells from the miniature Webley, shoved the Webley in the man's pocket, turned him about and shoved him to the door. "In a word—scram!"

The man turned, smiling with his shell-like teeth. "Would five thousand dollars interest you?"

"A thousand would, but what's that to you?"

"I have a friend who would pay you five thousand dollars for that little oblong strip of green, watermarked paper."

"I work for a living," Cardigan said, "and the agency I work for has a reputation. I don't think it would go nuts about doing business with you."

"But how about you?"

Cardigan took three long strides and gripped the little man by his shirt front. "Who the hell are you?"

"Please don't get pugilistic," the little man said in a tranquil voice.

Cardigan turned about with him, hurled him across the bed. "I've been here only twelve hours," he growled, "and I'm getting fed up on a lot of people."

He straddled the man, held him down by the throat with one strong hand, used the other to go through his pockets. He pulled out a wallet, keys, some envelopes. Getting back on his feet, he said: "Now stay there," and began sifting the articles.

Presently he shrugged, tossed the lot back on the bed. "You can go," he said. "And tell that lousy tabloid you work for that they couldn't buy me for a hundred thousand! And mark me, little morning glory! If you go monkeying around here again things may happen to you. Out—and goom-by!"

The little man rose, patted down his clothes, picked his derby from the floor and bowed at the door. His shell-like teeth gleamed. He backed out saying nothing, closed the door quietly.

When Cardigan went downstairs fifteen minutes later, Massey, the house dick, headed him off.

"What did that reporter from the tab want, Cardigan?"

"A short autobiographical sketch, Mr. Massey. Something like 'From Plowboy to Mastermind.' I said mine wasn't interesting. Referred him to you."

"And for that you gave him a split lip, huh?"

"He stubbed his toe and fell against a radiator."

"Yah!"

"Goom-by!"

Cardigan ate breakfast in the coffee shop, went out carrying his topcoat under his arm. Under the facade, he looked up and down the street. Across the way, diagonally, a man stood in front of a Western Union window. Cardigan walked west, turned south into Sixth, used a store window as a mirror and saw the man follow him.

He turned around abruptly and retraced his steps, putting a cigar in his mouth. The man who had followed had no time to duck. He slowed down, however. Cardigan came up to him, stopped, said: "Got a match, brother?"

The man was young. "Sure," he said, and passed a packet.

Cardigan lit up, returned the packet, said: "Spider on you!" and struck the man's lapel lightly. Beneath the cloth he felt the hardness of a police shield.

The man looked bewildered.

"Give Lieutenant Strout my love," Cardigan said, and rolled on, puffing enthusiastically.

The plainclothesman did not follow.

CHAPTER THREE

The Girl in 616

TEN minutes later Cardigan got out of a taxi in front of a six-story apartment house. He pounded a broad flag walk and tramped in through a broad, imposing entrance. The livery of the negro elevator boy hurt his eyes.

"How is every little thing?" Cardigan grinned.

"What floor?"

"All right, be dignified— Six, colonel."

The elevator rose in silence. Cardigan got out at the sixth floor and walked on carpets resilient as sponge rubber. He stopped, raised a bronze knocker on the black door of 616, let it fall back.

A girl with a shock of blond hair opened it and looked at Cardigan with wide, baby-blue eyes. She had on blue pajamas and a blue peignoir trimmed with sand-colored old lace.

"Yes?" she chirped in a babyish voice.

"I have grave news for you," Cardigan said with a judicial air.

"Oh—what?"

Acting fatherly, he took hold of her hand, patted it with rough tenderness the while he worked himself through the doorway and kicked the door shut. He scaled his hat into a velours divan, grinned broadly at the girl. She shrank back, drawing her peignoir about her small, rounded body.

"What—what do you want?" she asked, fear tailing her words.

Cardigan grinned. With his ungodly shock of hair and his heavy, powerful shoulders he filled the room. He indicated a love-seat.

"Sit down, Miss Callahan."

"W-what d-do you—"

He suddenly crossed the luxurious living room, looked in the bedroom, the bathroom; turned and regarded the girl across the length of the room.

"Now let's put the cards on the table, sister. I know who you are and what you are, so don't try to pull an act on

r throw a faint or in any way try
id me into believing that you don't
w what it's all about. I may look
a gorilla, but I'm not going to
n you down. All you have to do
nswer a question."

The baby-faced girl swallowed.
-what is it?"

"Who cashed that twenty-thousand
ar check for you?"

Miss Callahan sat down on the love-
sinking into one of its twin cush-
. She gripped her knees with white
ds the nails of which were lac-
ted in red. Her baby-blue eyes
ted. She looked innocent and hurt.
Come on, come on," Cardigan
wled, thumping across the carpet.
was big, towering, inimical in a
her-faced way.

The girl made a sound that sounded
"Eek!" and drew her knees up to
breast, gripping her ankles.

"I—I don't know what you're talk-
about," she cried in a tiny, breath-
voice. "I—I d-don't know you.
at right have you got to come in
? You b-brute!"

"For God's sake sister, don't pull a
k line like that. I tell you I know
. I know you got a check for
nty thousand. I know you cashed
and not in a bank."

She jumped to her feet and began
ing up and down dramatically.
his is an outrage!" she cried. "I
't know you and I don't know what
're talking about. You forced
r way in my apartment and if you
't leave right away I'll call the man-
ment and we'll see Now—" she in-
ated the door—"get out!"

"Tone down, girlie!"

She stamped her foot. "Get out!"

He grabbed her. Her eyes popped
the flat of his hand stifled a scream.
hair stood up on his nape. He
ok her.

"You fool! Pipe down!"

"Release the lady, Mr. Cardigan."

Cardigan stiffened, twisted his neck.
The reporter from the tabloid stood
with his back to the door holding the
small Webley and smiling with his
shell-like teeth.

"Naughty, naughty!" he mocked.

Cardigan released the girl. She
reeled away from him, bounced into the
love-seat and lay panting and choking
out hysterical little sounds.

"So," grunted Cardigan, his big
hands hanging at his sides, his face lowering.

"Just so, Mr. Cardigan. Observe
the steadiness of this gun and act ac-
cordingly."

"Cool, ain't you?" Cardigan
growled.

"As the proverbial cucumber."

"N-now who are y-you?" cried the
girl.

"Your benefactor," said the little
man. "I eavesdropped." He smiled
politely at Cardigan. "You'll be
going directly, won't you, Mr. Cardigan?"

Cardigan felt the red color of chagrin
flooding his face and neck. He felt suddenly oafish in the presence of this cool
little man with the gun and the steady
hand. He crossed to the velours divan,
picked up his hat. He kept looking at
the girl and backed up toward the door.
In a mirror back of the divan he could
see his own and the little man's image.
The little man was behind him, holding the gun, smiling.

Cardigan's right elbow shot back-
ward and upward. It caught the little
man neatly under the chin and snapped
his head back violently to the tune of
clicking teeth. Cardigan jumped to
one side and pivoted at the same time.
His fist traveled a foot and smashed
against the little man's chest. The little man slammed against the wall so

hard that he rebounded and ran into Cardigan's short left. That straightened him momentarily. The gun dropped from his fingers. Glassy-eyed. he went down like a balloon suddenly deflated.

Cardigan picked up the gun with one hand and with the other drew manacles from his pocket and lunged at the girl. The leveled gun cut her scream in the bud. He drew her from the divan, made her sit on the floor and manacled her to the unconscious little man.

"Now be quiet," he said huskily.

He began searching the room. He turned out all the drawers in a high, narrow secretary. He found a bank book showing a deposit of twenty thousand dollars two weeks ago. He scanned letters. He ransacked the living room and the bedroom with a vengeance. In the bedroom he knocked over a vase of flowers into a pink waste basket. Cursing his clumsiness, he picked them up, and spotted a small card and a small envelope lying in the waste basket. The card had written on it: "Just a remembrance for a favor from you know who." A plain white card such as florists supply. And on the accompanying envelope, printed in green, on the flap: "The Shelman Florist."

Cardigan pocketed card and envelope and went back into the living room. The girl was shivering.

Cardigan said: "This guy here works for the daily tabloid, so look out for him. Why the hell don't you tell me who cashed that check and get the benefit of silence? Do you want to have your name sprawled all over the papers?"

"I w-wish you'd leave."

"You little scatter-brained fool, they'll use you eventually! This guy is looking for the same information I

am, but he wants to spread it in t[] tab."

"I——have nothing to say."

Cardigan shrugged. He bent dow[] unlocked the manacles and put them i[] his pocket. He threw the Webley o[] the velours divan, started for the doo[]

"B-but this man!" cried the gir[] "What am I going to do with him."

"Try ice bags or smelling salts. wouldn't care."

He opened the door, went out, dow[] the corridor. He punched the elevato[] button and went down with the stony faced negro.

THE Shelman Florist Shop was i[] the small arcade of the Shelma[] Hotel. It was a small, chic cubicl[] with a floor of lozenge-shaped tiles. Th[] attendant was a girl in a black jerse[] ensemble. She smiled brightly an[] Cardigan took off his hat, leaned on th[] black marble counter.

"If I asked you in a nice way miss, would you tell me who sent flowers t[] Miss Roberta Callahan, 4111 Danne[]ford, in the last day or two?"

"Strange request, isn't it?"

"Strange as strange. How about it?"

"I don't know." She tapped her foot and kept throwing little glances at him. "It's unusual. I never had it happen before. I don't know what to say. Who are you?"

"By one look at my ugly map couldn't you tell I was detective?"

"No."

"You're being kind. I am."

She blushed. "Wait a minute."

She went to the rear of the shop, looked through a file of carbons. In a minute she returned. "I'd like to keep my name out of this," she said.

"Sure thing."

"They were ordered by a Mr. P. K. McHugh."

Cardigan went out finding the air a
eeter thing to breathe. P. K.—Pat
McHugh, the boss of the old party.
t McHugh sending flowers to Rob-
a Callahan by way of remembering
favor she had done him! Pat Mc-
igh, arch-enemy of the reform ticket
l Mayor Evan Holmes——

On his way back to the Flatlands
rdigan picked up three different
vspapers, went to his room and read
m. Last night's murder was front-
ge stuff. The dead man had finally
en identified as Carl Dorshook, alias
arles Dorn, alias James Matson.
s record went back to Toledo, Chil-
othe, Dayton, Pittsburgh and Balti-
ore. According to the police, how-
er, he could not be linked up with
y local mob, though apparently he
d been. Theft of the mayor's car
larged the headlines and evoked a pic-
re of the mayor in each paper.

Cardigan tossed the papers aside and
ought things out. He knew the po-
ce were not through with him yet.
e knew they couldn't hang anything
a him but he also knew that they
uld make things uncomfortable for
im. He wanted to protect himself, to
eer away from any hint that he was
orking for the mayor.

He went out and took a high-speed
ain out to a suburb five miles dis-
nt. From the telegraph office at the
ilroad station he sent a code message
the main office in New York. Trans-
ted, the message said:

In a jam. Send a long wire. Make
it a follow up on a fake case to kid
the cops. Use your own judgment.

He gave the address of the Hotel
latlands. He suspected that Massey,
he house dick, would get a copy of it,
nd he wanted it so. Because Massey
ould turn it over to Lieutenant Strout.
le took the tram back to the city and
t one o'clock he received a message.

The girl may also be using the
name of Sterrit. Her hair is dark
red instead of brown and she was
last in Cleveland, not Springfield,
Ohio. She has stenographic ability
and can also play on the harp. If
there is any place of amusement
there featuring a harpist look into it.
She affects an English accent and has
a complex for using big words such
as amanuensis and gymnosophist.
Her parents are desolated, so show
results and spare no expense in ob-
taining same. If you feel you need
the assistance of another operative
let me know.

George Hammerhorn,
President,
The Cosmos Detective Agency.

Cardigan appreciated the message, excepting the nonsense about the harp.
Certain that the mayor's wire was being
tapped, he walked six blocks to a Postal
Telegraph office, wrote out a message
and saw a messenger depart with it.

He was in his room at two o'clock
when Otto Shreiner, the mayor's chauffeur knocked. Cardigan put him on a
chair.

"You can help your boss and me in
a big way," Cardigan said. "At midnight I want you to come here to my
room and stay here for an hour while
I'm out. The night telephone operator
comes on duty at that time and she's
never heard my voice. At a quarter
past twelve I want you to call her and
ask her the time. At twelve-thirty I
want you to call the Union Station and
ask the best train to St. Louis tomorrow
forenoon. At a quarter to one I want
you to call the operator again and ask
her to call you at eight in the morning.
Got that straight?"

"Yes, sir."

"Try to speak like me. You know,
rough, as if you owned the place or
something. Get me?"

"Yes, sir."

"You took a room here all right?"

"Yes, sir."

"What room and what name."

"I signed Henry Josephs of Indianapolis. Room 411."

"O. K. Stay in your room and use the stairs on the way down."

"I used them on the way up."

Cardigan slapped his back. "You'll do, Otto!" Then he let the chauffeur out.

The tabloid, Cardigan knew, had no political stand, no moral stand. It had a personal grievance against Mayor Holmes dating back to a day six months ago when the mayor, in a radio speech, had called it "a filthy, depraved rag"; this because two of the tabloid's reporters had broken into the home of a woman whose daughter had been slain in a love tangle. In an effort to steal photographs and letters, they had bound the mother and precipitated a nervous breakdown. On the other hand, the Press-Clarion was politically definite in its stand against Holmes, carried considerable heft in the south and east ends. and obviously would jump at the opportunity to undermine the mayor's character.

Cardigan knew for certain that the tabloid was after that check. He had a strong hunch that Pat McHugh possessed the check. And he wondered if The Press-Clarion had a finger in the pie too. The murder of Dorshook was an accident—a bad one. It was reasonable to suppose that some mob in the extortion racket had got wind of the check, had wanted Cardigan for purposes of extracting definite information. Thus Cardigan had three distinct groups of enemies. And he was hampered by the police.

CHAPTER FOUR

Strong-Arm Stuff

AT three o'clock he went down to the lobby for the afternoon edi-tions. He was on his way across to the newsstand when he saw Strout and Blake come barging through the swing doors. He sensed trouble. A savage doggedness was in Strout's gait and manner and Blake wore a wily, bitter smile.

"Now don't give me any back talk," Strout chopped off. "Over to headquarters with you."

"What's this—another one of your bright moments?"

Blake gripped Cardigan's arm. "Ixnay on that back chat."

Cardigan looked disgusted. "Wait'll get my hat and coat."

Blake shook him. "You come right along!"

"You go chase yourself. I get cold in the head easily."

Strout muttered: "We'll go up with you."

In his room Cardigan took his time. "What have I done now?"

"Snap on it!" Blake clipped.

Cardigan picked up Hammerhorn's wire. "Have you seen this?"

Strout read it, looked up at Cardigan with his muddy eyes, looked down at the wire again. Then he tossed it on the bed and said: "Come on."

Cardigan said: "D'you know of any place around here featuring a harpist?"

Blake took a crack at Cardigan's ribs, from behind. Cardigan, whirled, cursed, his eyes blazing, but Strout grabbed him from behind. Blake snickered and went to the door, opening it, and Strout marched Cardigan out. They went to headquarters in a taxi.

In a dusty office on the second floor a uniformed cop sat in one chair and the negro elevator boy from the Danneford Avenue apartment house sat in another. His eyes got round when Cardigan looked at him and then Blake ocked Cardigan into a chair and uckled loosely.

"Is this the guy?" Strout said to the gro.

"Yassuh."

"O. K." Strout sat on the desk, angled one leg and turned his horse ace to Cardigan. His eyes got mud-ier, his face dark and dour. "Now pout, big boy."

Cardigan knew it was no time for orseplay. He saw in Strout a good op, a hard one, short on speech and ot a man to be kidded when he was a deadly earnest. Blake was a wind ag, but he could be nasty too in a mean, sly way. The presence of the negro was hint enough that something had gone wrong at the apartment house. More properly, in Roberta Callahan's apartment.

"Spout about what?" Cardigan asked.

Strout indicated the negro with a nod. "This guy described you to a T. The minute he described you I knew it was you. You called on a girl named Roberta Callahan this morn-ing. Right?"

"Tell me some more."

"All right. When you came down in the elevator the boy here says you looked red and mad and mean. What the hell were you doing in Roberta Cal-lahan's apartment."

"What proof have you I was in her apartment?"

"There are eight other apartments on that floor. We asked the occupants of those apartments if they'd had any callers. They hadn't."

"I thought the Callahan girl might have told you."

"She couldn't. She's in the hospi-tal."

Cardigan felt a chill knife his spine. His brows bent. "Was I the only guy in her apartment?" he snapped.

"The boy says you were the only man got off at that floor before ten-thirty. She went out at ten-thirty. At two o'clock she was picked up on a road near the Wabash, unconscious. She was beaten up. She has a black eye and a fractured jaw and we don't know if she'll live."

Blake shook his fist. "By cripes, Cardigan, you can't pull off a thing like that!"

Cardigan glowered. "You horse's neck, do you think I'd beat up a wo-man? Outside of my personal habits in a job like that, d'you think the agency'd stand for it?"

"Listen," said Strout dully. "I don't know you except from what I've seen of you. You've been handing us the run-around since you hit the city. Now what the hell were you doing in her apartment?"

Cardigan folded his arms. "You read that wire, didn't you?"

"What of it?"

"I was on a tip that the girl I'm tail-ing was seen in the company of Rob-erta Callahan. I went there and saw the Callahan girl. She got touchy be-cause I busted up her sleep and we had an argument. I was mad because I thought she knew something about this girl and wouldn't tell me. She finally threatened to call in the management if I didn't take the air.

"As I was about to leave a man called on her and I didn't want to make a scene, so I left."

"Who was the man?" Strout asked.

"How should I know?"

"What did he look like?"

"Kind of small, I remember. It was dim in the room and I didn't bother to look at him close enough."

Strout looked at the negro. "I thought you said he was the only man got off that floor before ten-thirty?"

"Yassuh."

Strout looked back at Cardigan. "Well?"

"Well? Well, they have a staircase in that place, haven't they?"

"Why the hell should anybody climb six flights when there's an elevator?"

"How should I know? Either the dinge is lying or the guy climbed the stairs."

"I ain't lyin'," growled the negro.

Blake chattered, "It's this guy's lying! This big bum right here! I know his kind! He can keep a straight face all he wants but he's lying! He's a lousy two-faced liar! There's only one way we can make this baby talk!"

Strout looked at Blake absently, looked back at Cardigan. Blake jumped on Cardigan where he sat, planted a knee in Cardigan's stomach and gripped his throat with both hands. Cardigan wore a cold, crooked smile.

"Spring it!" Blake rasped.

Cardigan chuckled. "Nuts."

Blake struck him across the face with an open palm. The chair creaked. Cardigan jammed his hands under Blake's armpits, rose mightily and sent Blake sprawling across the desk. The negro yelped. Blake fell to the floor, carrying a chair down with him. He came up spitting oaths and drawing his blackjack.

Cardigan was set for him. Strout turned and blocked Blake, took the blackjack away from him and shook his head. Blake cursed. Strout shook his head and shoved Blake into a chair. Strout dropped the blackjack to the desk and looked dourly at Cardigan.

A windy glitter was in Cardigan's eyes. "You pipe this, Strout! I've got a lot of power behind me and a lot of money—enough of both to make you and this whole police department take water! And as for that fathead partner of yours, he'll get his jaw broken if he tries any rough stuff on me.

I'm no heel! I'm no cheap back-alley gangster! I work for a salary and it's damned small considering what I have to put up with. And unlike you guys I get no graft."

"Shut up," said Strout.

"I'll shut up when I damned well feel like it! If you—listen, Strout—if you want to pinch me, go ahead and pinch me. You haven't got a thing on me. You know damned well I wouldn't beat up a woman. You pinch me and I'll be out inside of three hours. And what can you pinch me for? Because some heel tried to take me for a ride? Because I called on a girl who later was taken for a ride? Damn it, I've got a reputation! A big one! And not in any hick town, either! And I should throw a fit over a couple of hicks like you and Blake? You'll pinch me—yes, you will!"

Strout colored. "Can't a man ask you a question?"

"Oh, that's what you call it! That's what you call busting into my hotel room last night! That's what you call falling on me in a hotel lobby! That's what you call dragging me down here like a red-hot! Oh, what big eyes you have, grandma!"

He bent down, picked his hat off the floor, punched it back into shape and slapped it violently on his head.

"I'm going out of here," he said. "and I'd like to see you stop me. And I'd like to see you come around and bother me again. I'd just like to see you!"

He yanked open the door, shot Blake a look of scorn and banged out.

AT eleven that night Cardigan walked into the Flatlands lobby, bought some tobacco at the newsstand. He asked for mail at the desk. There was no mail, but another fake wire from

Hammerhorn supplementing information on the "runaway girl."

"I have to work in my room tonight," he told the clerk. "And I don't want to be disturbed by anybody."

On the way across the lobby he ran into Massey.

"I hear they had you down to headquarters," Massey said.

"Did you ever hear the story about a hotel detective who solved a great murder mystery?"

"No."

"You never will."

Cardigan went up in the elevator, checked his wrist-watch with the elevator boy's, said good night, and strode to his room. At a few minutes to twelve Otto Shreiner came in and Cardigan impressed on him the necessity of making the three telephone calls. Then he put on his coat, turned up the collar, and pulled his hat down low on his forehead.

He went downstairs by the stairway. The stairway was enclosed, with a door on each floor, and was really a fire-escape. It terminated near the side entrance of the hotel, and Cardigan left unobserved and put his head into a brisk fall wind. The city had very little night life, and what it did have was not obvious. Cardigan used darkened store windows for mirrors and walked three or four blocks to make certain he wasn't being followed.

Roberta Callahan was still unconscious. Cardigan knew who had given her that beating—or pretty nearly knew; the little man from the tabloid. What Cardigan did not know was whether the beating had served its purpose and extracted information. Lester Sisson was the little man's name. Had he given her the beating alone or had he hired strong-arm men?

Cardigan hopped in a taxi and gave a West End street corner as his destination. Ten minutes later he got out and watched the taxi speed away. The wind clapped the skirt of his overcoat smartly. The sky had a wintry look, with tattered scud driving across the moon. The wind threshed in a big sycamore tree and telephone wires hummed. Cardigan got his bearings and moved up a wide, deserted street where substantial houses stood far back from the sidewalks.

He crossed an intersection and kept on. He saw the tail-light of a parked car halfway up the block. He crossed to the other side of the street. He walked with long, purposeful strides. He looked across the street at the car because he heard its big powerful engine purring softly. There was something familiar about the car. It was a big touring, with the curtains up. He looked straight ahead. Fifty feet farther on he turned his head to the left and looked at the fieldstone house of Pat McHugh. It was dark.

Cardigan kept on, turned left into the next cross street and did some quiet and deliberate cursing. He was sure it was the car that had opened fire on him, killing Dorshook. Its presence in the street meant one of two things; either the men were friends of McHugh or had come on a mission similar to Cardigan's. If the latter, were they certain McHugh had the check or, like Cardigan, were they taking a chance?

Cardigan stopped, looked up and down the street then scaled a low stone wall. He went through shrubbery in the rear of the corner house, fell over a croquet wicket in the back yard of the next and then came to a waist-high hedge that blocked the way to McHugh's grounds. He followed the hedge to the rear of the yard, squeezed between the end of the hedge and the stone wall it met there. He went back of McHugh's double garage and peered around the corner of it at the rear windows of the house. The hatchway to the cellar was open. The garage was empty, doors open.

He had not been able to see how many men were in the car. He did not know how many were in the house. He ducked from the garage to the hedge and crept along in the shadow of it, nearer the house. He stopped, kneeling, his hand closed on the gun in his overcoat pocket. He looked at the illuminated dial of his wrist-watch. It was twelve twenty-five.

A couple minutes later he saw a shape materialize out of the hatchway. A tall man, topcoatless, dressed in dark clothes. He stood for a moment listening, a gun in his hand. Then he took hold of the open door, let it down slowly, softly.

Cardigan made the dozen feet in three long steps, jammed his gun against the small of the man's back as the latter was rising.

"Quiet!" Cardigan muttered.

The man froze in a half crouch.

Cardigan whispered, "Stick your gun straight up in the air—arm high. Quick!"

The man's arm went up. Cardigan took away his gun, put it in his own pocket.

He said: "You should have dumped that car right after you bumped off Dorshook."

He could see the man's muscles flex, heard a breath being sucked in sharply. The man started to turn around.

"No you don't!" Cardigan muttered.

"Who the hell are you?"

"A reporter from The Press-Clarion. Now hand it over."

"Geeze, looka here now——"

"Hand it over!"

The man whispered an oath, put a hand in his inside pocket, passed an envelope over his shoulder. Cardigan took it, put it between his teeth, drew out a smooth oblong of paper with his left hand, then shoved it and the envelope into his pocket.

"Now walk toward that garage," he said. "Along the hedge here, then across."

He kept behind the man, prodded him with the gun. He knew that if Roberta Callahan died he would have a tough time of it with the police. They had no proof against him but they could raise an unholy row, hold him if they had to and create a lot of undesirable publicity for the agency. In which event Cardigan knew he would stand a good chance of losing his job. He had to protect himself. He walked the man to the garage entrance and told him to keep walking till he reached the back wall. While the man did this Cardigan swung the doors shut, slipped on the lock, snapped it.

He heard the man jolt the doors a second later, heard him mutter fiercely: "Damn you, what you doin'?"

CHAPTER FIVE

Cardigan Crashes Through

CARDIGAN looked at his watch. It was twelve thirty-five. He backed away toward the shadow of the hedge. He had almost reached it when he heard a twig snap. He pivoted, saw a man standing by the side of the house.

He heard "Burt!" called in a hoarse whisper. He remained silent, motionless. Again—"Burt!" A little louder, almost stronger than a whisper. And eager—anxious.

After a moment the man moved cautiously into the rear yard. He looked at the closed hatch doors, at the rear of the house. He moved again, peering hard. He was nearer the garage now.

Again he called, "Burt!" in a whisper.

The man in the garage answered in a whisper. "I'm in here! Get me out! A guy got it!"

The other tensed, went swiftly to the garage. "Got it!"

"Yeah!"

"Who?"

"A guy from The Press-Clarion. Cripes, get me out!"

"Sh!" the man on the outside cautioned, and stood in a tense listening attitude. Then he examined the lock. "I'm damned if I can open it."

"You gotta! You get me outa here! Here! There's no windows— only the door here—"

"Quiet—quiet, loud mouth! . . . Lemme think . . . Hell, I can't force it—"

"Take a chance! Put a couple o' slugs through it! That egg— Listen, Louie—that egg knows I was in on that Dorshook kill. You gotta get me out. I ain't gonna fall for no rap on my lonesome. You get me out or you and Joe and—"

"O. K. Get back outa the way. I'll blow her off, then lam. Better not hang together. We'll join up at Cicero's—and don't you make any more cracks who takes a rap and who don't. O. K.—get back."

"Hey you!" Cardigan said in a low, blunt voice. "Scram!"

The man called Louis almost fell over with surprise.

"And watch that rod in your hand," Cardigan said. "You heard me—beat it!"

The pitch of his voice and the darkness made it hard for Louie to locate him. Louie began backing away.

"Louie!" cried the man in the garage. "Louie, you ain't gonna leave me here!

So help me, if you lam out on me I'll shoot the whole works!"

Louie stopped. He looked over his shoulder. Another man was coming along the side of the house. He stopped and looked at the cellar hatch, then at the shape of Louie.

"Say," he whispered, "Sisson's gettin' nervous. He says we better breeze. There's at patrolman due through here any minute."

Louie backed up toward him, and the latter whispered, "Where the hell's Burt?"

"Louie!" Burt cried in a hoarse whisper.

The third man began: "What the hell—" Then Louie made a motion of his head, kept backing up.

"Come on, Joe," Louie whispered grimly.

"But Burt's in that garage! How— Say, what's the matter?"

"Come on, you fool."

"I'm gonna get Burt!" Joe lunged toward the garage.

"Scram!" Cardigan barked. "You heard what your pal said."

"Louie!" Burt pleaded.

Joe stopped in his tracks, made a half turn with his gun held low. Its muzzle whipped flame and thunder through the dark. Cardigan heard the bullet snap through the hedge. He fired the gun he had taken from Burt and the echoes barked among the houses.

Louie's gun exploded. Cardigan heard the snick of the bullet passing, the slap of it against the stone wall beyond. He threw a shot at the dim shape of Louie and ruined a drain pipe on the house.

Joe began yelling, "My God—my God!" and ran toward Louie. Burt hammered inside the garage.

"I'm hit!" Joe gasped. "I'm hit, Louie!"

Cardigan snapped: "You guys beat it!"

Joe, yelling, "Oh, I'm hit bad!" ran right past Louie, fell over a flower bed and squealed like a woman. Louie backed up swiftly, cursing. There was the sound of a motor roaring, of gears being meshed savagely. Joe got up out of the flower garden and looked toward the street.

He cried: "Sisson's ditchin' us, the louse!" He hefted his gun, yelled: "Hey, wait!" and staggered wildly toward the street. The touring car roared past in second, slammed into high violently.

"Hey!" screamed Joe; then— "You dirty—" Rage choked him. He raised his gun. Flame burst three times from the black muzzle.

"Good cripes!" Louie moaned. "Come on, Joe—come on!"

Rubber tires rasped on the rough pavement. The touring car slewed from left to right, blindly, like a harried animal. Then suddenly it headed for the curb. The chassis wrenched at the springs as the car hurtled over the curb. A sycamore ripped off the left rear mudguard. A low iron fence met the front tires, ripped them open. The radiator crumpled. The iron fence crumpled and the big car crashed head-on into a stone house. Glass snarled. The rear tires heaved five feet off the ground, slammed down again. The rending sound of tortured metal raked the streets for blocks.

Joe and Louie reached the sidewalk.

"Help me, Louie!" Joe gasped.

"Come on—run!"

Louie set an example but Joe found it hard to follow. He reeled along, coughing. Louie ran faster.

"Louie—lemme a hand—"

But Louie ran faster.

Joe fell down, braced himself on one arm. "Louie!!" he cried savagely.

"You hear me!" He raised his gun. He fired. Louie swerved, hit a tree with such force that he bounced back and crashed down in the middle of the street.

CARDIGAN wiped off the gun he had taken from Burt and tossed it in front of the garage. He passed back of the garage, crossed the two yards, paused an instant by the stone wall and then vaulted it and landed on the sidewalk. He strode swiftly away. Stopped once to hide behind a tree and watch two cops rush past, then went on. Five minutes later he boarded a city-bound trolley. He looked at his watch. It was twelve minutes to one.

It was three minutes to one when he got off, four blocks from the Flatlands, and entered an all-night drug store. He crowded into a telephone booth, called police headquarters. He pitched his voice high.

"You guys down there—take this or leave it. There's a red-hot in the garage back of 906 Magnolia Avenue. He was one of the guys bumped off Dorshook. . . Who am I? Santa Claus to you, brother."

He hung up, left the drug store and walked to the Flatlands. At one he slipped in through the side entrance, ducked to the stairway and started climbing. At two minutes past one he entered his room.

"O. K., Otto. Beat it."

"Did you get it?"

"I did," Cardigan said. "Quick. Back to your room."

He rushed Otto out. Then he whipped off his clothes, got into pajamas, rumpled his hair, grabbed a magazine and climbed in bed. He took one look at the mayor's check, chuckled, slipped it in the back of the magazine, tore the envelope to bits and dropped them in a waste basket.

He put the magazine under his pillow. He reached for his briar pipe.

The clock's hands crept around to two. The hotel was quiet. Vagrant street sounds rose sharply. No one disturbed Cardigan. He knew that headquarters must be throbbing with activity. Surely Sisson had been killed in that crash. Press wires were humming. Still the hotel remained quiet. Cardigan yawned, turned off the lights.

Strout came in with Massey bright and early next morning while Cardigan, suspenders draping his hips, was lathering his face by the bathroom mirror.

Cardigan bowed elaborately.

"Swell morning, Strout!"

"Not so swell. Say, a guy named Sisson: Massey said Sisson paid a call on you once here."

"Oh—you mean that little morning glory from the tab. Yeah, he did. He'd heard about me and wanted my picture for the tab. See that rug in there? Well, he tripped over that and busted his lip against the radiator."

Strout looked mournful. "Sisson got bumped off last night."

Cardigan stropped his razor. "Too bad."

"It was funny. Two other guys got bumped off—they bumped off each other apparently. There was a third guy locked in Party Boss McHugh's garage. It was very funny. There was a fourth guy that slopped up the other's parade. The guy in the garage said he said he was from the Press-Clarion."

"Reporters turning gangsters, huh?"

"That guy was no reporter."

Cardigan said: "How did the girl make out?"

"She died."

"You're here to make a collar?"

Strout shook his head. "No. Just before she died she identified the guy we found in that garage as one of the men. On the way out of the hospital the guy pulled a fast one and broke loose. We had to shoot him."

"What was all the fireworks around McHugh's house?"

Strout pawed his jaw. "Well there was one guy knows all about it. The fourth guy. And the fourth guy was the guy made a phone call to headquarters at a few minutes to one this A.M. And a gun we found was the one that did for Dorshook. Our ballistics man checked up."

"And what's that to me?"

Strout wore a bleak smile. "It's funny—how that mysterious phone tip cleared you up completely. The guy said he was Santa Claus."

"And I suppose now you're going to call me Santa Claus!"

"There are a lot of things I'd like to call you, Cardigan. But just now I'm too tired. You're in the clear now. O. K. But whatever job you are on—if I catch you in this town after tonight—"

"You knew I was leaving this morning, didn't you?"

Massey looked uneasy.

Strout turned and walked to the door. Massey opened it and went out first. Strout turned and stared sourly across the room. Cardigan, patting his face with a hot towel, grinned.

"Go ahead—grin!" growled Strout.

"Ain't I?"

"Sure."

"Grin!"

"Ain't I?"

"Damn it, laugh your head off!"

"Ho-ho! How's that?"

Strout disappeared, banging the door.

Cardigan hurled the wet towel at the door, heaved into the bathroom chafing his hands in high good humor and bursting into a lusty ballad of the levees.

Make It Snappy

by

Erle Stanley Gardner

Author of "Snowy Ducks to Cover," etc.

*Eyes wide with horror, Ed May watched those growing pools of crimson
through the half-open door. The men had been brutally slain and now
the killers were forging his own name to the murder confession, were
pressing his fingers upon the bloody knife hilt—before they took
him and that beautiful mystery girl for a death ride!*

A cry showed that he had been seen. The darkness spat a stream of ruddy fire than fanned his cheek.

CHAPTER ONE

The Signet Ring

E D MAY didn't like the man's face. The eyes were too close together, the lips too thin. But the lips were quirked into a smile, and the eyes blinked, then squinted, as the smile crept up the face.

"Mr. May?"

"Yes," said May.

"I'm William Proctor." It was a simple statement made in a voice that was altogether too purringly honeyed.

"Good evening, Mr. Proctor,"

snapped May. "You wish to see me?"

"About the ring you advertised," said his visitor.

"Oh," said Ed May. "Come in."

He stepped to one side, holding the door open. His visitor walked in, and Ed May felt some subtle sixth sense amplifying the instinctive recognition of impending danger which had flooded him ever since the man's face appeared at the door.

He decided, however, there could be no possible opportunity for the man to make trouble. But his dislike made him tense and businesslike.

"You saw the ad, you say?"

"Yes. The lost and found in The Tribune."

"You acted quickly then, because the paper has barely reached the street."

The smile left the thin lips. "That's my business. The ring's important— to me."

Ed felt his face flush.

"No need to get hostile," he said. "You'll have to describe it."

"Easy. Two interlaced triangles on a lady's signet ring. That should show you it's my property."

Ed shook his head.

"The ad would have told you that much."

The visitor sneered. "Initials S.P. engraved on the inside."

Ed May grudgingly acquiesced.

"You're right. Guess that entitles you to the ring."

He started for the drawer of the writing desk. The telephone rang and he scooped the receiver to his ear.

"You the man that put the ad in the lost and found department of The Tribune?" asked a rasping voice.

"Yes," he said. "And there's a man here who has called to see about it."

The voice rasped raucously in his ear.

"Don't do anything about that ring until we get there. This is police headquarters. We're sending a detective right up."

Ed's surprise was reflected in the unthinking exclamation which burst from his lips.

"Police headquarters! Why, what under—"

And he stopped, abruptly aware of the beady eyes which were fastened upon him, realizing that his visitor was tense with anxiety.

"O.K.," he said.

"Right up," said the voice, and there was a click at the end of the line.

Ed May hung up the receiver and turned back to the man who had given the name of William Proctor. The thin lips had ceased to smile. The eyes glittered dangerously. A deft hand flipped a roll of bills from the pocket.

"Here's a hundred dollars, reward and expense. I want the ring."

Ed May sparred for time.

"I'm afraid I'll have to get a little better description."

The visitor moved uneasily in his chair.

"What do you want?" he asked, but there was a rasping tension about the voice which gave Ed May his warning.

Of a sudden, as well as he had ever known anything in his life, he knew that this man was about to pull a gun. And he was unarmed. Moreover, he was well across the room from his visitor. He thought quickly. He realized he would have to get to closer quarters. He walked toward the man.

"Well," he said, reaching his right hand into his jacket pocket. "Here's the ring, but——"

The other sensed his purpose. The man's right hand flickered into a swift arc of motion, and Ed May found himself staring into the business end of an automatic.

SO certain had he been that Proctor intended to make this very move, that it seemed to him he had lived through this scene before at some other time in his life. Then the illusion fell from his senses, and he recognized the menace of the glittering eyes, the purpose which gleamed from them. The man was contemplating murder!

"So the police rang up!" sneered Proctor. "And you're stalling for time, eh? Hand over that ring, and be quick about it!"

May kept his right hand in his jacket pocket, fumbling. He was wearing a signet ring on the third finger, and it was none too tight a fit. He worked his fingers, and slipped the ring off.

The thin lips parted to speak once more.

"If your right hand don't come out of that pocket clean and pretty, you're going bye-bye!"

May had an uneasy feeling that he was destined to go bye-bye anyway. Proctor only wanted to get possession of the ring. Then he intended to silence Ed May's lips. He realized there was far more to this ring business than had appeared on the surface.

He felt the signet ring slip off his finger. He took his right hand out of his pocket, tossed the ring to the surface of the table across which Proctor sat, and in such a manner that it would roll.

Proctor's glittering eyes fastened upon the golden band in greedy appraisal. The left hand shot out to retrieve the ring. The gun in the right hand wobbled.

Ed May went into action with the savage speed of a cornered panther. He crashed against the table, flung it up and over. Proctor was caught by the edge of that table. He whirled, clawed at the polished, slippery, slanting surface, strove to bring the gun around.

Ed May's left crashed to his jaw.

The edge of the table pinned Proctor to the chair. May's right clamped down upon the gun. He tugged, wrested the grip loose. Proctor's chair crashed to the floor. May jumped back. The gun had skidded from their grasping hands, slid down the table, and was on the floor. May started to run around the table.

Proctor slid down, got to hands and knees, and darted out into the clear. May came toward him, unafraid. Hand to hand, in equal combat, he felt he was more than a match for the slender figure of his caller.

But Proctor had had enough.

He flung the table about so it impeded the other's rush, and went through the door of the apartment on the run.

Ed May barked his shins on the table, trying to follow Proctor and sprawled his length on the floor. He scrambled to hands and knees in a running crawl, staggered to his feet, reached the outer door and found the corridor empty.

The man who had given his name as William Proctor had reached the stairway.

MAY grunted his disgust, went back into his apartment, picked up the table and looked at the automatic. The identifying numbers had been filed out. The gun was fully loaded, ready for business.

He thrust it in the drawer of the table, then walked to his mirror, straightened his tie, and ran a pocket comb through his hair. A peremptory knock sounded on his door.

Two broad-shouldered men hulked on the threshold.

"Mr. May?" asked the man in the lead.

"Yes," said May.

"You're the one that put the ad in The Tribune?"

"Yes."

"Headquarters," said the man, and pushed his way into the room, walking with purposeful determination. The other followed at his heels, pausing only to kick the door shut.

Ed May motioned to chairs.

"Sit down."

"Nope. No time. Wanta take a look at that ring. Think it was stolen. Have the initials S.P. on the inside of it?"

"Yes."

"Sounds like the one. Where'd you find it?"

"On the sidewalk on 150th Street."

"Know about where?"

"Yes. It was opposite the entrance of an apartment house. The Belleview, I think it was."

"Uh huh. That's the ring, where is it?"

"Here," said Ed.

"Let's see it—what's that on the floor?"

May followed their pointing finger.

"That's a ring I took off. I'd better tell you about it. There was a man here when you telephoned. He heard me say police headquarters, and he pulled a gun on me."

The shorter of the two men interrupted. They seemed in a terrific hurry, these men.

"Yeah, that can keep. Let's see that ring you found. It's important."

Ed May felt that it was strange the two detectives showed no more interest in his visitor who had pulled a gun to enforce his demands, but he produced the ring, a slender band of gold, terminating in a plain face upon which had been engraved interlaced triangles.

"Yeah. That's the one all right."

The taller man reached for it and dropped it casually in his pocket.

"We'll take it along. Let you hear from us later."

"The cost of the ad?" asked Ed May.

One of the men carelessly pulled a roll of bills from his pocket.

"Got change for a hundred?" he asked.

Ed May remembered the hundred dollar bill that Proctor had taken from his pocket. He looked over on the floor. There it was, crumpled, lying where it had fallen when he upset the table.

"No. I don't need it. There's a bill this man Proctor left. I want to tell you about him."

The broad-shouldered man thrust his roll of bills back in his pocket.

"No time now. See you later."

"But he acted like the thief!"

"Yeah? It'll keep. Come on Fred."

They pushed their way out of the door.

"Listen here," said Ed May, "I should have some sort of a receipt for that ring."

"Aw, go jump in the lake!" said one of the men over his shoulder, and they started for the stairs.

Ed May flushed, started after them.

"Look here, I don't give a damn whether you're the chief of police and his right-hand assistant. I'm going to have a receipt."

He stopped. The men, starting swiftly down the stairs, had paused to look over the rail. Two pairs of broad shoulders were visible, hulking upward upon a swift run. The men May was following, stopped, exchanged glances, and turned as with one motion.

One of them muttered something in a low voice to the other. The shorter man nodded. "It's the only chance," Ed heard him say. They they hurried back toward him.

"Sure, sure," soothed the taller man.

"You're entitled to a receipt. Come right in and we'll make one out!"

Ed May hesitated. That second of hesitation was fatal. A blackjack thunked down upon his skull. He felt a sudden nausea. His knees crumpled. He was grasped by strong hands. He was not unconscious, but he was unable to coordinate his muscles. They picked him up like a baby, rushed him back into his own apartment. One of them whipped a handkerchief from his pocket and thrust it into his mouth.

CHAPTER TWO

Double Murder

ED MAY tried to struggle and could not. Things were whirling around in a giddy dance of reeling confusion. His mind seemed to be perfectly clear, but the room was looping the loop every time he tried to make any sudden exertion.

"Out?" asked one of the men.

"Just about. Blow glanced. Stick him in the bedroom. I'll watch him. You do the stuff. They don't know you, but, for God's sake, don't let 'em see me."

Ed May was hauled into his own bedroom, flopped down on a bed. The shorter of the two men stood over him. Ed noticed that the heavy hand held a businesslike automatic trained on the crack in the door which led to the sitting room. The other hand held the handkerchief in Ed's mouth.

There was a knock on the outer door.

"Good evening," said the voice of the taller man.

"Hello," answered a booming voice, "are you Mr. May?"

"Yes. You're the detectives who were coming up?"

"Yes. The sergeant said you men-tioned some man being here about the ring. We're anxious to find out about him as well as to get the ring. Where'd he go? You said he was here."

"Yes. It was a mistake, though. He couldn't identify it. That is, he was looking for another ring that his wife had lost and he thought it might be the one I had. I don't know why. The rings didn't look alike."

Ed May heard the sounds of shuffling feet, of chairs scraping out, of the door closing.

"Listen," said the voice of one of the newcomers, "the way you describe that ring in the ad, it may be important as hell, see? You've read about Stella Prade being kidnapped. We're searching high and low for her. Her old man's about ready to kick through with the seventy-five thousand ransom that the kidnappers are demanding.

"Now she had a ring that had two interlaced triangles on its face, and the initials 'S.P.' on the inside. Your ad in The Tribune mentions a signet ring with a peculiar geometrical design, and says the owner can have the same by calling here, paying for the ad and identifying the ring. Now if that's Stella Prade's ring, it's a clue and a valuable one."

The detective was interrupted by the man who posed as Ed May.

"I'm sorry, gentlemen, but that doesn't answer the description of the ring at all."

There was the sound of a sigh.

"Lemme see it," said one of the voices.

The room gave forth the sound of motion. Ed May tried to call out. He sucked in his breath, choked on the gag.

The man who watched at the door, turned, scowled, held the barrel of his automatic in a menacing position, ready to crash it down. Ed lay still. There came the sound of voices from the other room.

"Can't see how you figured this ring had a geometrical design. This is a straight signet ring with initials. Looks like E.A.M. to me."

"Yeah," said the man who posed as Ed May, speaking easily and glibly. "I thought the ad was sorta funny myself. I gave the ring to the girl in the want-ad department and told her to make an ad about it. She told me how much money to give her, and I gave it to her. I never did see the ad until the paper came out a little while ago. I thought maybe—Say, I wonder if it ain't just an error on the part of the girl in the ad office. Maybe she put my address on some one else's ad. Maybe there was two rings found! Then she described the other ring over my name, and my ring in another ad."

One of the detectives grunted.

"Well, that might happen all right. Let me keep this ring for a coupla hours. We'll go down and get hold of the jane and see what she has to say. Funny way of describing this ring."

There was a pause, then the voice spoke again, rasping with suspicion.

"Hell, these might be your initials— E.A.M. Say, what——"

The comment was a signal for sudden action. The man who had been standing guard over Ed May jumped for the door. His gun was thrust through the aperture.

"Stick 'em up, and stick 'em up high!" he snapped.

ED MAY could hear a sudden gasp, silence, then the sound of motion.

"Get their handcuffs, Fred, handcuff 'em together."

One of the detectives spoke.

"Say, listen, you guys, you're get-
tin' in bad. What was the idea of puttin' that ad in the paper anyway?"

Ed May's ears caught the sound of a sudden blow, the scuffle of feet, a grunt, a thud, then the noise of a body pitching to the floor.

"Don't shoot, Fred. The knife!"

A man started to cry out. The cry was arrested in a peculiar gurgling sound. Again there sounded the thud of a blow. Something fell, jarring the floor.

"You've killed him!"

"You're damned right I killed him. He saw me. Think I can afford to be mixed up in this business?"

"How about the other one?"

"Is he dead?"

"No."

"Well, he will be!"

Ed May's horrified senses caught the thud of another blow, then silence.

The telephone rang.

"Answer it, Fred."

"Hello . . . . hello" said Fred's voice. "I'm sorry, just moving a little furniture around. We're done now. Sorry, ma'am if it disturbed the baby. You won't be bothered any more. G'bye."

The receiver clicked on the hook.

There was the rasp of a key in the lock as one of the men locked the door. Ed May strained his senses to listen.

"We're sure in for it now!"

"They was askin' for it. We got a bum break. That damned guy nearly copped Proctor. Lucky we were in the car with him. It was your bright idea, goin' up and posin' as the cops."

"Well, we had to do something, fast. There'll be a hell of a stink over this."

"There'd have been more of a stink if these dicks had run us into headquarters. You, with a murder rap waiting for you in Chicago. Me, with a death sentence standing out against me in California. Soon as they fingerprinted us we'd have been gone."

"Well, that ain't doing anything. What are we going to do now?"

Ed May took a deep breath, spat out the gag, rolled over to slip from the bed. The springs creaked, and the sound was audible to the two men in the room. He rolled to the floor, felt a spell of dizziness, staggered for a few steps, and found his eyes staring into the dark hole of an automatic.

"No, no, don't shoot. He's groggy. Cut his throat."

There was a flash of a knife.

Ed May tried to scream. The sound was nothing but an abortive gurgle. A heavy hand had clamped itself in his hair, jerked his head back. He caught the gleam of a knife, felt his throat bared to the blade.

"Hey, wait a minute!"

"Huh?"

Ed was held, too weak to struggle against the grip, his head thrust back, the knife almost at his throat.

"If we kill this guy the cops will put the whole thing together."

"Well?"

"If we take him along with us they'll do some wondering. They won't have too much of a line on what it's about. You're a good penman. You look around and find some of his writing. We'll forge a note, leave it with the dicks, see? The note'll say that he committed a murder five years ago and the dicks were about to find it out so he had to kill 'em."

The man with the knife snorted.

"The bulls won't fall for that line of hooey. They know about the ad in The Tribune. That's what brought 'em up. And remember old Prade is spendin' money like water. He's got an army of detectives."

"Listen, do what I say. It'll mix things up and throw 'em off the track. You cracked that old jane in Salinas. You can dope up a swell confession and

forge this guy's name to it. They'll telegraph the California police and get an answer back that the murder was done just that way. That'll make the confession look O.K. They'll start huntin' this guy, May, for murder.

"Then we'll take him out somewhere, hang him to a tree limb with a forged suicide note, sayin' he's trapped and he ain't goin' to be taken alive."

The grip on Ed May's hair slowly released.

"Maybe there's something to it. We gotta get out of here, though."

"Sure. Maybe we can get Prade to."

"Listen, guy, we can't get Prade to do a damned thing. We're goin' to go out and croak that broad. She'll talk if they ever get her back. With the murder of those two dicks we're in a hot spot. We gotta save our skins."

"How about Bill Proctor?"

"He's a rat. We won't let him know what happened. We'll tell him everything went off jake. Then we'll croak him when we get ready to start. He'd turn State's evidence if he knew it was a frying job. The other one that's guarding the girl is O. K. We can take him along. He's wanted in Nevada and he'll keep quiet."

"I told you not to—"

"Say, what the hell is this? A debatin' society? Get busy and pen out that confession. Look around and find some stuff that's got his writing."

The gag was thrust back into Ed May's mouth.

"Sit down, you!" snarled a voice in his ear.

ED tried to make his knees obey the command. A vicious blow thudded into his stomach. He caved, sank breathless to the floor.

"Kick him in the face," said one of the men.

"Naw. Ain't he got to walk out?

We don't want to have to carry him. Stick a rod in his back and make him walk. Have Proctor drive around and pick him up in the alley. We'll run him outa the back door under his own power."

"O. K. Let's get that confession."

Ed May gasped for breath, writhed with the pain in his stomach. He could hear the rustle of papers, the scratch of a pen.

"Put it on thick, about how you choked her for her money and she croaked on you, then you searched the place and couldn't find the coin."

"Say, who's writin' this confession, anyway?"

There was a hoarse snicker.

Ed May's eyes saw double. They refused to focus properly; but he was dimly conscious of silent forms, soaking the carpet of the apartment with a welling pool of red, and he knew they were the two detectives—dead.

"Now stick his fingerprints on the knife and leave it here. Better get a fingerprint on the confession. That's a good job you've made of his signature!"

Ed May felt the fingers of his right hand pried open, then something warm and sticky flooded his fingers. He jerked the hand back in horror. Another hand clamped his wrist, pulled the reluctant fingers back, pushed the hilt of a knife against them.

"We're makin' an artistic job of this," said one of the men. "I wouldn't doubt if we got the police all balled up."

"Not for long."

"Maybe, but they'll never connect us with it—if we croak Proctor and the broad. It's a frying job now if we get caught, and we may as well go ahead and fix things so we won't get caught. We can kill a dozen as easy as one and they can't fry us but once."

"Well, let's go. I'll go get Proctor around to the back of the apartment."

A gun was thrust into Ed May's ribs.

"Listen, guy, you're goin' to walk out, an' you're goin' pretty. All you've got to do is to make one false motion, and you'll get your insides filled with lead. Get me?"

Ed May said nothing.

"Get on your feet."

For a brief instant, Ed May felt that he would force their hand, that they wouldn't dare to use the gun. Then the two grim and silent objects sprawled on the floor bore mute witness to the fact that these men were in deadly earnest. While they might wish to avoid the noise, if possible, they wouldn't hesitate to shoot if necessary.

He lurched to his feet.

"That's better," said the man who held the gun. "We're goin' the back way. You know the ropes. Don't try anything."

The gun jabbed.

Ed felt himself pushed toward the door. His feet were uncertain, but, with every step he took, he managed to get his muscles under better control. He went through the door, into the long, dim corridor, steadied himself by touching the tips of his fingers against the wall. He kept going until he found the back stairs.

There was a friend of his in the apartment that was just on the corner of the stairway. Ed was letting his fingers drag along the wall. He had but to drum them across the thin panels of the wooden door and his friend would come to see what was causing the sound.

Then—and the thought of what would then happen caused Ed May to pull back his hand. After all, it was his own funeral. No need to implicate his friends in the thing. The man with the gun would shoot. It would simply mean two dead men instead of one.

They went downstairs. Somewhere below, a door opened and a young woman, attired for the street, stepped into the corridor.

"Remember," hissed the man.

Ed May walked steadily.

"Good evening, Mr. May," she said, and eyed him somewhat curiously.

He bowed formally.

"Good evening," he replied, and tried to make his voice sound casual. She paused, as though inviting conversation.

The heavy-set man who held the gun stepped swiftly around him, stood still for a moment, ready to fire at them both, and Ed May gathered his strength, ready to sacrifice his life by leaping and holding the gun close to his own body, giving the girl a chance to escape.

She gave a little flounce when she saw that Ed May was not going to stop, turned and walked steadily down the corridor. Ed May resumed his march. The back door loomed.

"Open it," said the man at his back.

Ed pushed on the door. The welcome freshness of the night air cooled his forehead. He saw twin headlights in the alley, then the dark shape of an automobile purred up to the cement stoop where groceries and merchandise were delivered. A door opened.

"Any trouble?" It was Proctor's voice.

"Not at all. He was easy. We got all we came for."

Ed was pushed in on the seat. The face of Bill Proctor turned from the front seat, grinned at him.

"Thought you was pretty smart, didn't you?" he sneered.

One of the other men spoke sharply.

"Shut up!" he said.

Proctor turned back, sullenly. The car lurched into motion.

CHAPTER THREE

"Make It Snappy"

ED MAY felt the coolness of the night air, felt, also, the pressure of the gun that jabbed into his ribs. He knew that his life was to be forfeit in any event, but he felt that there was a chance if he could regain his strength, get that confounded dizziness out of his head.

The smooth motion of the car lulled him somewhat.

He fought against the blackness that seemed to well up from within him, but his senses would not function properly. Knowing that there was a respite granted him, he drifted into a condition of half consciousness.

The car rolled through the paved streets, hit the main boulevards, sang into increasing speed as it turned toward the suburbs.

They traveled for fully an hour, and Ed May had a chance to get something of a grip on himself. He was feeling better now. The thought was in his mind that he might be able to whirl and grab the gun from the hand of the man at his side, kick out with his feet, perhaps wreck the car.

But it was a forlorn hope, and the vigilance of the man at his side seemed never to relax.

The car slowed. There was no other car in sight in either direction.

"Right along in here somewhere," said one of the men.

The driver grunted, spun the wheel.

There was a dirt road under the wheels. The car swung away from the pavement, ran along a field that seemed to be given over to garden truck, then passed a cornfield, twisted through a patch of woods, and came to a long hay field. The hay had been cut and raked into regularly spaced piles. The fragrant odor of it seeped into the nostrils, giving a smell of freshness to the night.

The car swung again, this time to a narrower road which ran along the center of the field. There was a deep ditch on either side of the road. Abruptly, woods loomed ahead and the car went into a leafy tunnel.

They ran through the patch of woodland, came to a stretch of rocky land, turned to the right and a little ramshackle dwelling loomed ahead.

The car stopped.

"Better go in first, Fred, make certain everything's O. K."

The door opened. The car lurched as the man got from it to the ground.

"Want me to go in, too?" asked Bill Proctor.

"Yeah. Might's well."

The men vanished. Ed May heard a click in the door. The driver of the car turned out the lights. Velvety darkness enveloped the machine.

The one who had been left as a guard switched on a small light in the dash, took an extra clip for his automatic from his pocket, started thrusting shells into it until it was well filled. Then he turned out the light. An oblong of mellow light glowed from the house. A low whistle acted as signal apprising him that the coast was clear.

"O. K. guy. Get out," he said.

Ed May got to the ground. He was pleased to notice that there was a spring in his muscles, that his nerves felt the surge of returning life, but he was careful to stumble, stagger, clutch at the support of the car door, as though he still was unable to control his muscles.

"Hell!" said the guard.

He took Ed's arm, an arm that Ed was careful to keep limp and lifeless, piloted the captive up a short flight of steps, across a porch, through a door.

"Into the bedroom," said the one they called Fred.

Ed May was swung through a door, propelled into a room that had been used as a dining room. He realized that he was going to have to think fast.

"Make it snappy," said one of the men, and Ed May took his cue from that remark. He knew that he must be sufficiently snappy to outwit these men. He had nothing but his wits to rely upon, and his wits must save him, or he would have but a few hours to live.

HE saw that the dining table held a sugar bowl, a can of milk bearing a red and white label, a salt and pepper set, a checkered red-and-white table cloth. Ed May stumbled, lurched, sprawled toward the table.

"Snap out of it!" roared the man who was following him. He lunged out, caught Ed's coat by the shoulder.

Ed went limp, flung the full force of his weight against the other's grasp. The clutching hand slipped from the fabric of the coat. Ed crashed against the table, clawed at the cloth, pulled it off, went to the floor in a confused tangle of cloth, milk and sugar.

Curses rang in his ears.

But Ed had planned carefully. His right hand closed upon the pepper shaker. He rolled over, groaned, and, masking his moves with his body, unscrewed the top of the pepper shaker. There were running steps on the floor.

"What's the trouble?"

"Aw, the damned sap's punch groggy. He took a tumble."

"Croak him then."

"No. Not here. We gotta cover our tracks."

Pepper slid into Ed May's palm, a pile of dry, cool grains that gave him some reassurance. Bill Proctor walked into the room, chuckled.

"Charge him with damages," he smirked. "Make it a cover charge!"

And he laughed at his own joke.

Fred grunted. "Might's well do the whole business right here," he said, meaningly.

"No, no. Wait. Get this bozo up and into the bedroom."

Hands clasped Ed May's arms. He was lifted to his feet, half pushed, half dragged as those feet wandered aimlessly, taking futile, abortive steps.

"Leave Bill Proctor to guard him," said Fred significantly.

Ed was catapulted through the door, toward a bed. A door slammed. Bill Proctor gave him a final shove.

"Snap out of it, guy," said Proctor. "I owe you a couple, and I want you to be feeling good when I paste you."

He laughed at that, a vacuous, silly laugh.

Ed May knew that his part demanded that he continue to groan and act groggy. But there was something hammering at the back of his consciousness, an insistent echo of the words of one of the gangsters "Make it Snappy!" He knew that seconds counted, that minutes were priceless. He twisted himself around, stared upward.

"They're going to kill me," he groaned.

Bill Proctor's laugh was scornful.

"Ain't that too bad!"

"And you, too," groaned Ed.

The laugh ceased in a gasp of sudden enquiry.

"Huh?" said Proctor. "What are you talkin' about?"

"They croaked the two detectives," groaned Ed May. "It's a burning job now. They're afraid you'll turn State's evidence, and of course, they're afraid of me. They're going to kill us both and beat it."

Bill Proctor came toward the bed.

"What's that you say—they killed the dicks?" he said.

Ed May got a glimpse of Proctor's face. It had turned the color of putty.

"Sure they killed 'em," he said, and closed his eyes, as though fighting for strength. "What'd you think they were doing back there—serving tea?"

Bill Proctor came toward him, bent over him shook his shoulders.

"Snap out of it, guy! Snap out of it! Gimme the lowdown!"

Ed mumbled sleepily.

"Killed the detectives. Gonna kill me. Gonna kill you."

Bill Proctor straightened, looked about him, bent low once more.

"Listen, guy."

There were steps coming toward the door. Proctor whirled. The door banged open.

"Better tie that guy up."

Bill Proctor stepped slightly to one side.

"For God's sake, Fred," he said, "did you croak those dicks?"

THE steps came to abrupt pause. Ed rolled his head so that he could see, and eased the lids of his eyes up, leaving them partly closed. Fred was standing, feet apart.

"What are you talking about?"

"This guy says you croaked the dicks. That's a burning job. They fry people who kill dicks."

"Do if they catch 'em," sneered Fred.

"You know they catch 'em!" said Proctor. "They always catch 'em."

"Think so?"

"Yeah. You know it's so."

"So this guy's been talking, eh?"

"Sort of half groggy," explained Proctor. "Sounds almost like he was talking in his sleep."

"Does, eh? I know a swell way to fix that."

"But listen, Fred, did you croak the dicks?"

There was the sound of a coil of light rope dropping to the floor as Fred opened his hands, then moved his right hand slowly back toward his hip.

"Yes," he said, shortly, "we croaked 'em. What are you going to do about it?"

Bill Proctor flung forth hurried words.

"No, no, Fred, don't! I know what you're planning. Don't pull that rod. I won't talk, I swear I won't. I only wanted to know how bad it was. If I'm in it with you I'll see it through. I just wanted to know. That's all. You can't blame me for that. Fred! Fred! Don't pull that rod. You don't give me a chance. You won't have to rub me out! I promise! I swear!"

Slowly, remorselessly, as inexorably as fate, Fred pulled the gun from his hip pocket. Proctor's hands were outstretched. He moved toward the hulking figure.

"For God's sake, Fred!"

The hand raised the gun. Bill Proctor dropped to his knees.

"No, no, no, no!"

Fred brought the gun down with a snap of swift motion. Proctor's hands, raised to ward off the blow, clutched futilely at the sleeve of the coat, broke a part of the force of the blow.

The gun thunked on bone, and Bill Proctor moaned, swayed, sprawled his length on the floor.

Fred balanced the gun, considered the form of Ed May on the bed, sighed, stooped for the rope.

"Oh, Charlie, better look in here!" he called. "We gotta finish this thing now."

Ed May's hand which held the pepper was commencing to feel the irritating burn of the spice and starting to sweat. It was now or never. He

stirred and groaned as Fred approached him.

"Don't know whether to tie you up, or——"

He sat up.

"Oh my head!" he exclaimed.

Fred snapped up the gun. "Try a pill from this!"

May's right hand flashed out. The pepper went straight into Fred's eyes. Ed swung to one side. The automatic roared. The bullet missed him by inches. Fred cursed with pain, swung, fired again, blindly.

This time the miss was wider and Ed dove in.

He heard running steps. Fred was hanging on to his automatic with a grim grip. He was striking out with his left hand with blind blows. His eyes streamed moisture.

The other man was running toward the room. His steps were coming across the board floor of the dining room. There was no time to be lost, no time to struggle futilely for the possession of that gun.

Ed May tore himself away from the gangster's grasp, scrambled toward where Bill Proctor lay on the floor. His hands groped along the inside of the coat, found a shoulder holster, tugged an automatic from it. Bill Proctor stirred — moaned, clutched feebly at him.

Ed May heard a curse. He turned his head.

The coming of the other man had complicated the situation, nor was the complication altogether unfavorable. Fred, his burning eyes causing him intense pain, was swiping at his tear streaming optics with the sleeve of his left arm. His right hand held the gun ready.

The man in the doorway seemed at a loss to grasp the significance of the situation. He paused for a moment, then he rushed toward Ed, raising his weapon.

FRED heard the sound of that rush, raised his own gun and fired. The big gangster spun half around.

"No, no, you damned fool!" he roared at Fred. "You almost shot me!"

Bill Proctor got to his knees, screamed. Ed raised the weapon he had taken from Proctor, aimed at the electric light and pulled the trigger. The gun roared. The light crashed into darkness and he squirmed along the floor. The room was vibrant with moving bodies.

A blow thudded, then there was the sound of two men locked in struggle. A gun roared once, twice. A gleam of light marked the door of the dining room. Ed May went toward it, gun ready. He felt the floor sway and give under the weight of the struggling bodies.

Bang!

"You asked for it, you fool!" said a man's voice.

Ed couldn't tell which one of the men it was that had spoken those last words. He went into the dining room on the run, saw the front door, knew that the gangster's car was out in front, and started for it. Another man was shouting questions from another part of the house. It was no time to hesitate. Then a disquieting thought struck him.

The girl!

Stella Prade had been kidnapped, held for ransom. She had dropped her ring as a clue. Ed May had found that ring, advertised. That ad had brought police and gangster alike—but where was the girl? Had they left her in the apartment house in front of which he had found the ring, or was she held a captive in this isolated shack?

He swung away from the front door. It was a one-story house, an affair of boards, unpainted sides, curling shingles, weather-beaten, insecure upon its rotting foundations. It smelled with the odor of decaying wood, with the mustiness of mold. There wouldn't be many rooms.

He could hear steps thudding the wood floor as the man who had been shouting questions ran toward him. Figuring out the door through which this man would emerge, he ran toward it. The other beat him. Ed saw the door fling back, a black shape catapult into the room.

"What's the trouble?" asked the man, checking his steps.

He was short, pasty-faced, bony-shouldered. Ed had a glimpse of high cheek bones, black lack-lustre eyes, thin lips. Then he saw the gun swing up.

Ed pulled the trigger of his captured weapon and rushed forward. Both shots were clean misses. Ed's went high, but his charge swung him clear of the other's shot. Ed smashed his gun down in a swift blow. The other dodged. The gun caught him on the shoulder. He staggered back under the impact of Ed May's charging body.

Ed slammed home a right uppercut. It caught the pasty-faced man fairly on the jaw—knocked him back and to one side.

Ed May rushed for the door through which the pasty-faced man had come. He was conscious of running steps as someone raced from the bedroom and he heard yells which seemed to be in Bill Proctor's voice.

He kicked the door shut, found himself in a kitchen, turned and saw another door. He tried it. It was locked. He crashed his shoulder against it. The rotten wood shivered into a mass of splinters. It was dry, half decayed, and seemed to fairly explode under the impetus of his charge.

Ed raised his foot and kicked in as much of the door as hadn't splintered open.

CHAPTER FOUR

Flames of Death

A YOUNG woman was seated on a bed, arms and ankles bound, a gag in her mouth, watching him with eyes that protruded in horrified wonder.

Ed May plunged his right hand to his hip pocket where he carried his knife, transferring the gun to his left hand. The girl shivered when she saw the naked blade, then suddenly grasped his purpose and thrust forward her bound wrists.

The keen blade bit through the ropes. She turned her head so that the knot of the gag was within slashing distance of the knife. As Ed cut the gag, she shook her head violently and spat. The gag tumbled from her mouth.

She flopped back on the bed, raised her legs.

Ed cut at the bonds, heard the sound of steps in the kitchen, whirled and covered the splintered door with his captured gun. The man rushed toward the door, abruptly stopped.

"Back or I'll shoot," he shouted.

The man kept quiet. Ed thought the gangster might be stalking toward the door, or waiting in the kitchen, ready to shoot anyone who would emerge. There was a single electric globe dangling on a fly-speckled green cord from the unplastered ceiling. Reaching out, he turned the rubber key which acted as a switch, plunging the room in darkness.

He heard the man in the kitchen make a surreptitious move. He kept his own gun on the door.

"Come on," he said to the girl.

There was a cobwebby window which showed as a grayish outline against the black of the room. Ed swept a pillow from the bed, used it as a shield as he pushed out the pane of the window. His shoe rasped along the lower edge, trimming off the saw-toothed glass remnants. She thrust out one foot, paused.

"Are you—?"

Ed heard the rushing steps. He gave her a swift shove.

"Make it snappy!" he said.

She gasped, shot out of the window into the night, thudded to the ground. Ed dove after her, lit on top of her as she was getting to her feet. They sprawled into a confused tangle.

Ed squirmed free, looked up at the window. A dark shadow was hulking against it. Ed fired. The black shadow jumped back and to one side.

"You're no gentleman," said the girl.

"I don't aim to be," said Ed. "Come on."

She hesitated. He grabbed her arm.

"For the luvva Mike, make it snappy! Can't you see—"

He didn't even wait to finish his own sentence, but slid his clutching fingers down to her wrist, started on the run, dragging her behind him. The gangster's car loomed ahead in the darkness.

"Now get into that car and don't be a dumb egg!" rasped Ed May. "I'm trying to save you."

He dashed around one side of the car, vaulted into it, reached for the starter button. He didn't bother to open the other door for her, but started the motor purring into action, rasped in the clutch.

There was no time to back and turn. The space at the end of the road was too narrow to permit of a single turn. Hay field was on one side, a barnlike structure used as a garage and the house on the other end.

Ed May simply charged the car into the hay field. He was conscious of the woman on the running-board, tugging at the door catch.

"I can't get this door open!"

He was busy with the steering wheel.

"Hang on then!" he called, and left her on the running board while he jolted out into the hay field, back to the road. The field was just a small neck of cultivated land between the rocky outcroppings, and the car jolted, jumped, lurched.

"I'll lose my hold!" the girl screamed.

SOMEONE fired from a window of the house, and the bullet zinged into the metal body of the car. Another shot apparently was a clean miss. Then half a dozen shots spat out in spiteful succession.

Ed saw they were shooting at the tires, waited momentarily for one of them to go flat. But the car was gathering speed. He heard the girl scream.

The wind was whipping her hair. Her light skirt was blowing up and slapping back and forth in the wind of their progress. The car lurched around a turn, shut out the view of the house, and the shots ceased.

Ed May slowed the car.

He opened the door. The girl slid along the running board, thrust her legs into the car, reached the seat. The door slammed shut. Her hands instinctively went to her garments.

"I think you're just about the rudest man I ever met!" she said.

Ed May kept his eyes on the road ahead, the throttle on the floorboards.

"Presume you're sore because I didn't call for you in evening clothes, or wait to send my card in by the butler! Ex-

pect you were waiting for me to come and open the door and hand you into the car, raise my hat, and walk around to get in—all the while those chaps were shooting at us!"

His tone was bitter. The car swept into a turn, skidded, straightened. He flashed a savage glance at her. To his surprise, she was laughing.

"That's the trouble with you big airedales," she said. "You haven't any sense of humor."

Ed was startled.

"Mean to say you were kidding me all the time?"

"Not at first. I thought maybe you were another gangster. You didn't say who or what, but just burst into the room and started rattling off commands and saying 'make it snappy,' 'make it snappy'. Then when you pushed me out of the window I got mad."

"What'd you hesitate for?" he asked.

"I knew where they had a gun hidden in that room," she said, "and I can use one. Thought perhaps we might need one."

Ed May flashed a startled glance back over his shoulder.

A car was coming down the road, headlights dancing in hot pursuit.

"We will," he said. "We're going to have competition. You're Stella Prade?"

He asked the question as an afterthought, as a matter of course.

Her eyes got big and round.

"What? Me, Stella Prade! Don't be silly! I'm Rose Hunt, the wife of one of those gangsters. We had a fight because he thought I was going to run away with Bill Proctor, and he tied me up!"

Ed May snapped his teeth together, slammed the throttle down on the floorboards until it seemed he would press a dent in the lumber.

'Well, of all—!"

He didn't finish. The road twisted and turned, leapt forward at him. Trees and rocks whizzed by, threatened to rip the body from the car. Once he struck a rock on the side of the road, skidded, rebounded, crashed into a tree, lost a fender, straightened out, and kept up his speed.

The car behind was gaining. The man at the wheel was driving like a crazy man.

The car burst out of the woods, into the main body of the hay field. It was a straightway here, but a road that was bounded by a ditch on either side. The car roared into greater speed, while the other machine dropped far behind.

THE girl turned, sat on one leg, surveyed the tense profile of Ed May, smiled, and peered back through the rear of the car.

"We're leaving them behind," she said.

"So it seems."

"Sorry you rescued me?"

He grunted. "What'd I rescue you from?"

"Probably a beating. My husband's awfully jealous. He'll hunt you down if you get away this time. You've got a gangster's moll on your hands. You'll have to support me now."

"Listen," snapped Ed May, but he never told her what she was to listen to, for there was a spit of flame from the car behind. That little pin prick of flame became a steady spitting of coughing explosions. Bullets whistled by, then started to hit the car. They sounded like hail on the tin roof.

"That's why they slowed. Getting a machine gun into action," said Ed.

There was a curve ahead. He swung the car.

The bullets rattled. Then, suddenly, a rear tire went out with a bang. The car lurched, settled, skidded. Speed was out of the question.

"Well," said Ed May, "that's the end. They're coming up with a machine gun. We can't make any speed, and—"

A thought struck him.

"Quick!" he yelled, and slammed on the brakes, jumped from the car. He was tugging a handkerchief from his pocket as he hit the ground.

The girl joined him. The pursuing machine was coming toward the turn fast.

"Meaning 'make it snappy!' I s'pose," said the girl.

"Shut up!" he told her.

His hands untwisted the gasoline cap, thrust in the handkerchief, pulled it out. A match scraped. The gasoline ignited with a flare of swift light. Ed May scooped an arm around her waist, started to run. They raced out into the stubble of the hay field.

The lights of the other car rounded the turn. The scream of brakes, the skidding tires, told of the attempts to stop it. A great cloud of dust was thrown up by the sliding tires, forming a mist about the headlights.

"Come on!" he yelled at her. "Can't you run any faster than that?"

"Let go my waist!" she said.

He released her. She raised her skirts. The slender well-formed legs flashed into speed.

"Come on!" she yelled.

Ed found that she was fleet of foot when she had a chance to run unhampered. The cloud of dust was clearing from the headlights of the other car. Ed plunged into a pile of hay.

"Come on!" he yelled.

She dove in, head first. Like two field mice, they began to burrow into the shelter of the hay pile.

"'Make it snappy!' I suppose you

mean," she said. "That's about all the conversation I've heard from you since I met you!"

He gathered she was mocking him, but was too intent upon what was happening.

The gangster's car had crawled up to within twenty yards of the burning machine. Bubbling gas was welling from the tank of the car he had driven, was flaming up with great red flames that crackled upward, sending fiery tongues into billowing clouds of black smoke. The conflagration spread rapidly, reddening the sky. The stubble commenced to burn, and a semicircle of flame crept out, growing wider, spreading faster.

Ed watched the two figures that were outlined for a moment, against the glare of the flames.

"They think we've raced on ahead. They can't get their car past on account of the ditch on each side of the road."

"Why didn't we?"

"Didn't we what?"

"Go ahead."

"Because that's exactly where they're looking for us. They've got a submachine gun. See it. There they go now!"

THE two shadows raced across the spreading circle of flame, ducked back to the road. There was the spatter of a machine gun as it swept the road ahead, then silence, broken only by the crackling of the flames.

The fire spread to the first pile of hay. That hay pile flamed into sudden brilliant light, disclosed the two gangsters, some twenty yards ahead of the car, the fire at their backs, searching the darkness.

The light also disclosed another shadow, hovering about the pursuit car.

"Looks like Bill Proctor had decided to throw in with them after all. They knocked him out with a sock on the head."

"Uh huh—they would!" said the girl. "Sorry you rescued me? You're in a gang war now."

"I was saving my own skin."

"You stopped to rescue me, though."

"Thought you were Stella Prade."

"Would you have rescued me if you'd known?"

He turned to look at her. They were both burrowed into the hay. The red glow of the spreading fire illuminated her features. This time there was no doubt of it. She was laughing at him, eyes dancing with little humor twinkles.

"No," he said, grinning. "I'd have asked your gangster husband to let me help beat you."

"You're so primitive," she remarked. "Listen, goosie, are you going to lay there until the fire creeps up and we go poof?"

"No."

"What are we going to do?"

"I don't know, but I have an idea. They think we're ahead of the car. I have a hunch. You stay here until the last possible minute. Then try to swing around ahead of the flames, but circle back the way we came. If you have to go through the burning stubble be sure to keep your clothes up where they don't catch."

"What are you going to do?" she asked.

"Try to capture their car before they get back."

"You can't back it up, and you can't turn around."

"No, but I've got another idea."

He jumped out from the haycock, started on an angling run, hugging the shadows which surrounded the fire as much as he could. The ruddy glow of the dancing flames were hot on his face. His shadow, coal black, danced grotesquely along the golden hay stubble. But he kept the flame between himself and the gangster car that had pursued.

Half a dozen of the haycocks were flaming at once now, sending colums of white smoke and red flame up into the sky. The gasoline was burning with billowing clouds of black smoke which were caught by the wind.

Ed May strained every nerve for speed, holding the automatic in his hand, stumbling occasionally over the hard surface of the dried ground, circling to keep back of the flames.

Then the flames gained too much. He had to go through them.

He took a deep breath, changed his course, and made a wild leap across the rim of fire, hit the smouldering heat of the burnt stubble.

The ditch yawned before him, a black stretch of inky shadow. A cry showed that he had been seen.

The darkness spat a stream of ruddy fire and a bullet whispered a message of cold death as it fanned his cheek.

He fired twice, fired from the hip, without checking his speed. The man who was standing by the gangster pursuit car, answered those shots.

The man who was firing at him shifted position. The light of the fire glowed redly upon a portion of arm and shoulder as they became visible from the shadows of the automobile.

Ed fired again.

Again the fire was answered. Ed charged onward. He heard something from behind him, a strangled gasping cry.

The girl was there. She had been following him all the way.

"I think I'm hit," she said.

THERE was no time to argue, no time to remonstrate for her foolhardiness in following him. Ed went on in his charge. He faced the barking gun of the gangster, caught him in his sights, pulled the trigger.

A dead, futile, hopeless "blick" announced that the gun was empty.

He flung himself across the inky ditches. Bill Proctor was struggling with a fresh clip of shells.

Ed was breathless. His muscles felt weak and nerveless, but he sprinted.

"I owe you one," he said.

Bill Proctor tossed away the clip, dropped the gun, set himself, swung a wild blow. It missed. Ed's charge terminated in a straight left followed by a right hook. He was winded. Both blows lacked timing. But they were enough for Proctor. He staggered under the impact, then started to run.

The fire had now fanned well out over the field. The red line of burning stubble was punctuated with white lights as chocks of hay flared up in fire.

Ed jumped into the gangster's car.

"Quick," he called to the girl. "Can you make it?"

She nodded, tugged at a door handle. Ed opened it for her and she floundered into the back, dropped to the seat.

"Where are you hit?" he panted.

"Shoulder—Don't mind me."

He heard the ripping sound of tearing cloth. Then he started the motor. He crept forward in low gear. The blazing car was directly ahead and the heat penetrated to the interior of the auto he was driving.

"Hold tight!" he yelled.

He jammed down the throttle. Flinging the car in reverse, he turned, thrust a head out of the window on the side.

The car went backwards. He knew that he must hold the wheel steady. To start wobbling would be fatal.

The road showed a curve. He tried to swing the steering wheel. He swung it too much, tried to correct the error. The car swayed, lurched. He slammed on the brakes. Too late. The rear which glinted the red firelight, was The car settled down.

Ed sighed, switch off the motor.

"That," he announced, "is the end!"

"I don't think so," she observed. "You've been too busy to notice what's happening. Look over there!"

A line of men, armed with guns from which glinted the red firelight, were coming charging through the red border of stubble fire.

"A police car," she said. "Stopped on the side road."

There came the spatter of coughing fire from the sub-machine gun of the gangsters. It was answered by a fusilade from the line of advancing police. The sub-machine gun became silent.

He turned back toward the girl. The firelight showed that she had ripped off her waist, and was bandaging a hole in her shoulder as best she could.

"Here, you can't do that. Let me."

He grasped the cloth, made a compress over the wound.

"Are you really a moll?" he asked.

"Of course not. I'm Stella Prade. But I thought you might be another kidnapper, you were so awfully abrupt. Get that bandage under the armpit there—that's it. Gosh, I'm wobbly—"

She slumped against him.

He held her close, felt the creamy smoothness of her satiny skin against his shoulder, looked at the fluttering eyes, the red lips, slightly parted, through which came her deep breathing. He felt an irresistible impulse, bent over, came to a hesitant halt with his lips but inches from hers.

The eyelids snapped up. He encountered laughing eyes.

"Make it snappy," she said. "Dad may be with those police, and he always was old-fashioned about kissing!"

TAKE IT FROM US!

YOU all know the old one about not being able to eat your cake and have it too. Take it from us there's not a thing in it!

When we began making plans for the first issue of DIME DETECTIVE MAGAZINE we were sure that a pretty satisfying thrill diet was in the mixing process. Then, when the knockout cover picture arrived and bang-up yarns from the finest writers of modern detective fiction began to pour in we knew that the various ingredients were in correct proportion and the oven at the right temperature. The finished product didn't let us down in our expectations any either. It was done to a turn, and one taste whetted the old appetite for mystery and action as had nothing we'd seen in ages.

It hasn't stopped there though, for this second layer has risen to perfection, and the one coming in January isn't going to fall down either. It seems that we've managed to concoct a feast that's going to keep growing in its capacity to thrill you and each succeeding course gives promise of filling the bill even better than the one before. You don't need to be afraid of eating this cake because there's more of the same where it came from and it's not going to run out!

LAST month we promised some more dope on the men who are making DIME DETECTIVE MAGAZINE the greatest action-mystery-adventure magazine on the market, so here goes.

Frederick Nebel, whose thrilling "Hell's Pay Check" you have just read, is— But let's let him introduce himself. He writes from Bridgton, Maine, and says: "Writing is my business, the one and only. It's no lark but on the

FREDERICK NEBEL

other hand I can think of worse jobs. I started from scratch, had some tough breaks and some good ones—and the tough ones fewer than the good. I've written almost every type of story. My first yarns were based on a pilgrimage I made to the Canadian Northwest, where my great-uncle was a pioneer. Once I shipped in a Norwegian tramp and knocked around the Caribbean. I've lived in France and in England. Was born in New York 27 years ago and spend about a month there every year. Like the city at night. There was a time when I worked on the waterfront.

"I react quickly to a Scotch joke or just straight Scotch . . . Masefield, Conrad, Rupert Brooke . . . a perfect motor

... Katherine Cornell ... white water ... the smell of coffee boiling over a woods fire ... summer fog ... a dark-haired girl (my wife) ... Charlie Chaplin. This could go on forever but I believe there should be a law against it.

"Six or seven months of the year I spend in Maine. The remainder of the year I go places and see things. Don't play tennis, bridge or marbles. Like pistol shooting but prefer the bow and arrow. Play a fair game of chess and a rotten game of poker. I can resist anything but temptation and I whistle in the bath tub."

That's all right as far as it goes but what we want to know is what he whistles. We'll try to find out for you before the next issue goes to press.

Erle Stanley Gardner's secretary writes from California that the author of "Make It Snappy" is having the time of his life in the Far East. He is making Manila his headquarters and is taking in Borneo, Saigon, and Sumatra. He plans to contact some head hunters in that country and we're all keeping our fingers crossed for his safe return. Singapore and the Malay Peninsula should furnish some interesting and thrilling material for his stories, and when he gets back we're going to try to persuade him to give us some mystery-adventure yarns with an Oriental background. They'll be worth waiting and watching for, so keep your eye on DIME DETECTIVE MAGAZINE during 1932.

HERE IT IS ....

_your first lesson in this popular, easy as A-B-C way of learning music

YES, learning to play your favorite instrument this thrilling new way is actually as easy as it looks.

Notice the first picture. The notes spell F-A-C-E—face. That wasn't hard . . . was it? Then look at the second E-G-B-D-F—Every Good Boy Does Fine. You can't *help* learning. All you do is look at the pictures and you know the entire scale!

Your next step is to play actual tunes, right from the notes. And all of the lessons of the famous U. S. School of Music course are just as easy, just as simple as that.

For by this remarkably clear course, you learn in the privacy of your own home, without the aid of a private teacher. No more tedious hours of dry theory or finger-twisting exercises.

Just imagine . . . a method by which you learn music in less than half the usual time, and at an average cost of only a few cents a day!

Easy As Can Be!

These fascinating lessons are like a game.

Everything is right before your eyes —printed instructions, diagrams, and all the music you need. You can't possibly go wrong. First you are *told* what to do, then a picture *shows* you how, and then you do it yourself and *hear* it. The best private teacher could not make it clearer or easier.

Forget the old-fashioned idea that you have to have "talent" or "musical ability." You don't at all, *now!* More than 600,000 people who could not read one note from another, are now popular and accomplished players, thanks to the U. S. School of Music.

New Popularity—Plenty of Good Times

If you are tired of always sitting on the outer rim of a party, of being a professional looker-on—if you've often been jealous because others could entertain friends and were always in demand—if you've wanted to play but never thought you had the time or money to learn, let the time tested and proven U. S. School come to your rescue.

Don't miss any more good times! Learn to play your favorite instrument and be the center of attraction wherever you go. Musicians are invited everywhere, they are always in demand. Enjoy this greater new popularity you have been missing. Have the good times that pass you by. You can have them—easily!

Free Booklet and Demonstration Lesson

Our wonderful illustrated Free Book and Free Demonstration lesson explain all about this remarkable method. No matter what instrument you choose to play, the Free Demonstration lesson will show you at once the amazingly simple principles upon which this famous method is founded. As soon as the lesson arrives, you see for yourself just how anyone can learn to play his favorite instrument by note in almost no time and at a fraction of what the old slow methods cost. The booklet will also tell you about the astounding new Automatic Finger Control.

Read the list of instruments to the left, decide which you want to play, and the U. S. School of Music will do the rest. Act NOW. Clip and mail this coupon today, and the fascinating Free Book and Free Demonstration Lesson will be sent to you at once. No obligation, of course. Instruments supplied when needed, cash or credit. U. S. SCHOOL OF MUSIC, 8612 Brunswick Bldg., New York City.

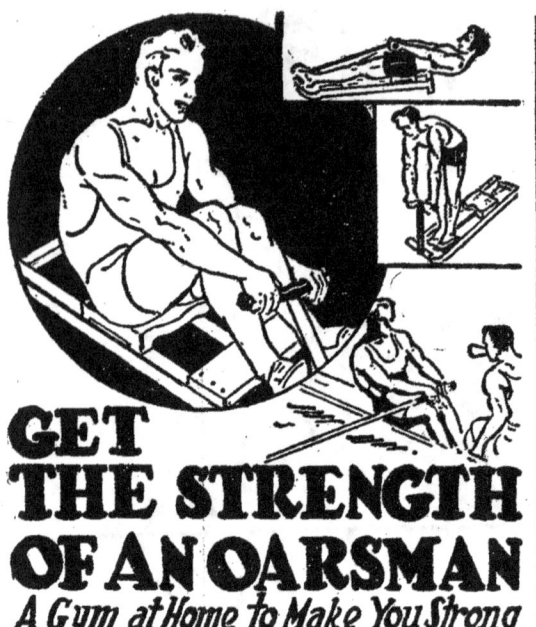
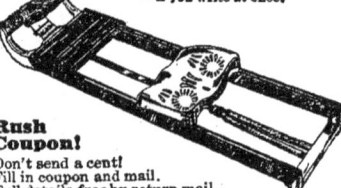

126

127

"Take me away from him!"

"Lock me up so I cannot escape—beat me if you like—and I will tell you all I know. But while HE is my master I will not betray HIM!"

Terrified, trembling, she crouched there—an exotic vision from the Orient—pleading with the stern-faced detective to save her from the fiend she called "Master!"

Who was this girl—whose rare loveliness stood out so richly against its setting of murder and deviltry?

Who was this Yellow Monster who plucked men from life and left no clue behind?

What were the strange bonds that made her his slave?

If you would join London's greatest detectives in unwinding this and many other equally baffling Oriental Mysteries—if you would match your wits against the most diabolical Oriental cunning ever conceived—then by all means send at once for <u>Your Free Examination Set</u> of

If you would enjoy exciting and unbelievable adventures as you plunge from the bright world of the West into the dubious underworld of the East—send for your free examination set while this offer is still open!

MASTERPIECES of ORIENTAL MYSTERY
11 Volumes of Matchless Thrills by SAX ROHMER

NO ORDINARY mystery stories are these, but the hidden secrets, mysteries and intrigues of the Orient itself!

Before your very eyes spreads a swiftly moving panorama that takes you breathless from the high places of society—from homes of refinement and luxury to sinister underworlds of London and the Far East—from Piccadilly and Broadway to incredible scenes behind idol temples in far off China—to the jungles of Malay, along strange paths to the very seat of Hindu sorcery.

PACKED WITH THRILLS FROM COVER TO COVER

Be the first in your community to own these, the most wonderful Oriental mystery stories ever published—books that have sold by the hundred thousand at much higher prices—books you will enjoy reading over and over again. Handsomely bound in substantial cloth covers, a proud adornment for your table or shelf.

These are the sort of stories that famous statesmen, financiers and other great men read to help them relax—to forget their burdens. To read these absorbing tales of the mysterious East is to cast your worries into oblivion—to increase your efficiency.

Priced for Quick Sale

Cutting royalties to the bone and printing these volumes by the hundred thousand when paper was cheap, makes this low price possible. But the number is limited; so mail coupon today!

Complete Sets Free on Approval

You needn't send a cent. Simply mail the coupon and this amazing set will go to you immediately, all charges prepaid. If it fails to delight you, return it in ten days at our expense, and you owe us nothing.

IF YOU ACT NOW!

A fortunate circumstance enables us to offer you free, as a premium for promptness, this beautiful 16-inch Karamaneh necklace of fine imported simulated light green JADE and small moonstones.

JADE is the semi-precious stone celebrated by poets and the delight of Chinese emperors.

The retail value of this lovely necklace is $3.00—but you get it free if you accept our offer now!

free!

THE MYSTERIOUS DR. FU MANCHU — SAX ROHMER Vol. 1
THE RETURN OF DR. FU MANCHU — SAX ROHMER Vol. 2
THE HAND OF FU MANCHU — SAX ROHMER Vol. 3
DOPE — SAX ROHMER Vol. 4
THE YELLOW CLAW — SAX ROHMER Vol. 5
TALES OF SECRET EGYPT — SAX ROHMER Vol. 6
QUEST OF THE SACRED SLIPPER — SAX ROHMER Vol. 7
GREEN EYES OF BÂST — SAX ROHMER Vol. 8
THE GOLDEN SCORPION — SAX ROHMER Vol. 9
BAT WING — SAX ROHMER Vol. 10
FIRE TONGUE — SAX ROHMER

McKinlay, Stone & Mackenzie, Dept. 130, 114 E. 16 St., New York City, N.Y.

www.ingramcontent.com/pod-product-compliance
Lightning Source LLC
Chambersburg PA
CBHW080911020726
47502CB00008B/2425

* 9 7 8 1 6 1 8 2 7 7 0 7 7 *